WAR OF THE GARGOYLES

War of the Gargoyles

Book One: Rebirth

Morgan R. Bramlet

Copyright © 2012 by Morgan R. Bramlet.

Library of Congress Control Number:		2012904285
ISBN:	Hardcover	978-1-4691-8061-8
	Softcover	978-1-4691-8060-1
	Ebook	978-1-4691-8062-5

All rights reserved. No part of this book may be reproduced or transmitted in any form or by any means, electronic or mechanical, including photocopying, recording, or by any information storage and retrieval system, without permission in writing from the copyright owner.

This is a work of fiction. Names, characters, places and incidents either are the product of the author's imagination or are used fictitiously, and any resemblance to any actual persons, living or dead, events, or locales is entirely coincidental.

This book was printed in the United States of America.

To order additional copies of this book, contact:
Xlibris Corporation
1-888-795-4274
www.Xlibris.com
Orders@Xlibris.com
110603

For my wife and kids, who are my world.
They inspire my creativity.

1

Kurt Riggins looked down at the young man clinging to the line twenty-five feet below him and couldn't help but smile. This was Troy's third major climb, and the eighteen-year-old was just learning how to shake off the nerves associated with being four hundred feet off the ground and having three hundred more to go.

At twenty-two, Kurt already had nearly six years of rock climbing experience under his belt and was qualified at expert level. He'd spent the last three summers crisscrossing the country with his college climbing club and taking on nearly two dozen walls and formations from Oregon's Joshua Tree to the Kentucky's Red River Gorge. In a few years he hoped to hit some of the more popular international destinations.

Standing six foot one inch and a wiry 155 pounds, Kurt possessed the ideal climber's physique. His tendril-like arms and spidery legs looked like a study in human anatomy, showing every cut and contour that defined his musculature. His skin was naturally tanned and weathered from years of outdoor recreation. Whenever he was in peak shape, as he was now, Kurt carried less than eleven percent body fat. His large nose, oversized ears, and a pointed chin gave him a somewhat gawky appearance, but his sharp blue eyes, thick blond brows, and short-cropped yellow-blond hair balanced his features in such a way to make it all work.

Having recently completed his bachelor's degree in international finance at Colorado State University, Kurt had already landed an entry level analyst position at the World Bank in Washington DC. In two more weeks he'd be heading off to start his career. But before he left for the new city, he'd decided to spend some bonding time with his little brother.

Growing up, Troy had tagged along behind his big brother like an energetic puppy. Whether it was skiing, hiking, kayaking, mountain biking, or some other activity, the little brother would always find a way to follow in the older's footsteps. When Kurt and a few of his high school buddies took up climbing, then thirteen-year-old Troy was too young and small for the dangerous sport. Instead he had to content himself to practicing on the homemade, thirty-foot-tall climbing wall they'd built with their dad in the backyard of the family's home. He eventually mastered the wall to the point that he could scale every level with his eyes closed.

When Troy was fifteen, their parents finally allowed him to go along on a climb with Kurt, on the condition that the teen was tethered between two experienced climbers. The intermediate level rock face was only 120 feet high, but it was more than enough to infect Troy the bug.

When Kurt headed back to college that fall, Troy got his own climbing crew together.

Following last year's growth spurt, Troy had grown from awkward teen into a heartthrob-handsome young man. He stood five feet eleven and a half inches tall, with a thin, athletic build that was just beginning to fill in. His shoulder-length blond hair, liquid blue eyes, and killer smile would make him even harder to resist as he got older. Even the popular girls at school, who'd brushed him off only a year before, had started taking notice of him. But high school was behind him, and Troy would be heading off to the University of Denver in a few more weeks.

At that moment both brothers were stuck flat against a towering, sun-warmed red rock formation like two insects. Their eyes scanned for prehammered pitons; their palms and fingers probed along the contours in search of the next handhold.

A favorite but somewhat isolated destination for expert-level sport climbers, "the Spire" was a seven-hundred-thirty-foot-tall, eighty-foot-wide formation that jutted straight up from the Arizona desert floor. Surrounded by the stratified, multicolored cliff walls of the canyon, the ancient red rock tower twisted and spiraled upward like an angry fist. The top of the formation was virtually flat and completely barren of vegetation. It was the ideal location to pitch a tent for an overnight stay under the stars.

Climbers who successfully negotiated the Spire would often post photos on their Facebook profile pages either standing triumphantly atop the summit or dangling their feet over the edge, drinks in hand. The endless desert vistas and rugged mountain ranges in the background made for a postcard perfect view.

"C'mon, slowpoke," Kurt hollered down to his little brother. "Or are you planning to have me carry you up the last couple o' hundred feet?"

"Shut up," Troy hollered back up. "I'm working it out."

Kurt chuckled to himself as he put both feet against the rock wall and leaned back in his harness so it supported him like a sling chair. He unhooked his plastic and stainless steel canteen and took a long, cold drink of water.

He looked down and saw his brother with arms and legs spread wide like an arachnid. The younger sibling was stepping up his pace.

"Work it out, little bro'," Kurt said to himself between drinks.

A sense of pride filled the more experienced climber as he watched his brother skittering up the rock wall, the teen's ponytail dangling from underneath his blue helmet.

It only took Troy a few minutes to catch up.

"Finally," Kurt joked. "I thought I was gonna be here all day."

"Yeah, yeah, laugh all you want for now, big bro'," Troy replied. "Just remember that as you get older, you're gonna get slower. So in a couple of years, you're gonna be trying to keep up with me, old man."

"That'll be the day," Kurt laughed.

He kicked off from the wall with his feet and, holding onto the line, swung in a wide lazy arc over about twenty feet to the right. The two brothers were now positioned parallel to one another on the wall.

Kurt called over, "Wanna race?"

"You know you'll beat me."

"How about I give you say a twenty-five-foot head start?"

At that, Troy smiled. Looking at the distance to the top, then after quickly running the math in his head, he literally licked his lips. "All riiiiight!"

The eighteen-year-old dug his fingers into his chalk pouch to get a fresh coating. Then he gripped a small outcropping and began pulling his body up.

Kurt shook his head as he watched Troy scampering upward. He'd also run the math in his more experienced head. He'd catch his little brother somewhere around fifteen feet from the top. But he'd let the kid dream for the moment.

Troy's body, which had been aching from fatigue, was recharged with a fresh infusion of adrenaline from the challenge. He couldn't wait to see the look on Kurt's face after he got his butt whipped.

Twelve minutes later Troy was poised about thirty feet further up the tower. His body was going crazy with the kinetic energy of excitement.

"Ready?" he called down. From the angle he could only see the top of Kurt's red helmet.

"Yep," Kurt confirmed. Then he shouted, "Go!"

At that, both brothers started up the wall. Their hands worked furiously searching out the optimal handholds and footholds, their eyes scanning the terrain above them, their heads assembling routes. Able to make his decisions quicker and execute the more aggressive moves, Kurt closed the distance between the two by ten feet within minutes.

"Man, you *are* slow," he yelled up.

"Shut up!" Troy laughed back as he tried to quicken his pace.

Just then a large, dark shadow moved across the tower, momentarily blocking out the early evening sun.

"What the hell was that?" Troy asked.

"What was what?"

"That shadow. It was huge."

"I didn't see anything."

"Something went right behind me."

"Maybe it was a plane."

"It wasn't a plane, dude. I know what a friggin' airplane looks like."

"Then an eagle or a hawk or something."

"That was way too big to be a hawk."

"C'mon if we're gonna camp up top, we gotta rock and roll. It's gonna be dark soon."

Troy settled back down. "Okay, okay," he said.

Both brothers turned their attention back to the climb.

For the next ten minutes Troy scaled at a pace that reminded him of the ease with which he moved up their old climbing wall. After visually surveying and mind-mapping the wall above, he'd mentally marked out a route that knew would get him up top in about twenty minutes. *There was no way Kurt was going to be able to catch him.*

"Prepare to be beaten by your superior, big bro." Troy boasted as he continued upward gaining in both speed and confidence.

After a few seconds, however, he didn't hear one of Kurt's usual comebacks.

"Did you hear me? I said, prepare to be beaten."

When there was no response again, Troy stopped to look back. He was sure that he'd see a grinning Kurt right at his heels, casually waiting to zip right by at the last moment and claim victory.

But Kurt wasn't right below him. In fact, he didn't see his brother at all.

"Kurt?" Troy called.

Nothing.

"Dude, I ain't gonna be tricked into stopping."

Troy knew from a lifetime of experience that Kurt had a knack for joking around. His brother had probably found a crevice to slip in or outcropping to hide behind and planned to mess with his Troy's head for a few minutes before laughing it off.

"Kurt! C'mon cut it out dude!"

Troy's eyes scanned back and forth across the tower, hoping to see Kurt's red helmet poking out from somewhere.

Nothing but a gentle breeze.

Several more minutes passed.

"All right, c'mon, Kurt!" he called again. "I know you're down there."

Thoughts of the unthinkable began to creep into Troy's mind. Mustering up the courage, he strained his moist eyes to look all the way down to the base of the tower. Rationally he knew that if Kurt had fallen he would have heard a scream. But he had to look down and see if he spotted his brother's broken and bloodied body on the ground below. He breathed a sigh of relief when he didn't.

The plan had been for them to reach the summit and then haul their gear up on a second line. After that they'd build a fire, eat some chow, throw out their sleeping bags, and spend the night under the clear sky and stars.

Then Troy thought to look up to the top of the Spire. Kurt was the better climber and could have taken a route that completely blew past Troy. He was hoping and praying that Kurt's gloating face would appear over the edge, looking down at him with a big, contented smile. They'd insult each other, share a laugh, and then Troy would climb the rest of the way to the top.

Nothing.

Talking mostly to himself, Troy said, "If you're just screwing with my head, Kurt, I swear I'll—"

It was then that he spotted the end of Kurt's line about forty feet away, slapping against the rock in the light breeze.

"Oh no," Troy's first instinct was to panic. "Kurt!" he yelled.

His heart beating like crazy, he started quickly pulling out his line to free up more length. He pushed off and swung over to the right, rappelling down about twenty feet as well. He grabbed up the ten-millimeter gauge black-and-orange braided climbing rope and examined it. It wasn't cut or frayed but had snapped clean.

"What the hell happened?" he asked himself.

If the line had been frayed, it would have meant wear or failure. If the end had been clean, it would have meant that Kurt had intentionally cut it with a knife. Instead the break was slightly ragged and uneven as if it had been pulled apart, which would have required more than a thousand pounds of force.

Troy was now completely befuddled and scared. He didn't know what to do, climb up and look from up top or rappel down and get to the jeep.

The sun was quickly setting, yielding the sky to darkness by the minute. The early evening breeze began whipping up. At the higher altitude the temperature was roughly ten degrees cooler and falling. By nightfall it was expected to dip below forty. Clad only in a T-shirt and shorts, Troy was starting to shiver from the cold.

"Kurt!" He called out, his cracking voice echoing unheard for miles.

Nearly fifteen minutes had passed since he'd last seen his brother. Somewhere in the distance, an old coyote howled at the moon. It was getting darker and colder, and Troy knew that he couldn't just sit there shivering and calling out. He had to make a decision.

Then he saw it.

It came out of the darkness, reflective eyes aglow, fangs bared, claws outstretched.

Troy didn't even have time to scream. Foot claws clamped onto the teen's shoulders, tearing deep into the flesh. Powerful batlike wings flapped in the air.

Kicking his feet, Troy desperately fought to hold onto the green-and-gold braided nylon rope.

"Help!" he cried.

Between his screams and protests, he heard the guttural grunts of his attacker. As he was being pulled away, the rope went taut and started sliding through his hands. He tightened his grip as hard as he could, holding on for life.

Two pitons were yanked out from the rock with a PLINK, PLINK sound, but a third piton caught and held. Panicking, Troy's eyes searched around frantically. He thought that if he could quickly reel himself in hand over hand, he'd be able to rappel down to the bottom and then make a run for it. His shoulders felt as if they were on fire, and he could feel thick, warm blood running down his chest and back from the open wounds.

The attacker pulled him hard again, and the line was speed ripped through his hands, burning through his flesh almost to the bone.

"Arrrghh!!" Troy cried as his hands let go in pain reflex. As the line fell away, his flailing hands fought to grasp the rope, which formed a lazy loop as it swung out of reach.

Having plucked its prey off the rock wall like a falcon snatching up a mouse, the predator tightened its purchase on the teen.

Terrified, Troy continued to squirm and fight. "Somebody help me! Help me!" he cried out at the top of his lungs.

The attacker responded with a violent whiplash-like shake. There was a dry, hard cracking sound as the teen's neck snapped.

Then the body went limp.

2

The battered white with brown stripe 1983 Winnebago Brave motored down the Arizona desert highway at a top speed of sixty-seven miles per hour. The vehicle was so loaded down with luggage, trunks, carriers, and souvenirs that even floored, it barely topped the speed limit on the I-40.

The passengers inside had spent most of summer break at various dig sites around southern Mexico and along the Yucatán Peninsula, taking in everything from well-known Mayan ruins to a recent excavation that had uncovered a potentially new species of dwarf sauropod.

At the wheel of the vehicle was Professor Adam Landis, PhD.

This was the fourth year that Adam had gone on the six-week-long expedition down south but only the third time he'd taken students along with him.

Three years ago, he had been elevated to full professor in the Department of Anthropology at the University of California at Berkeley. At the time, he was one of the youngest people ever to earn the distinction.

Two factors had contributed to Adam's meteoric rise in academia. First, he had been something of a child prodigy. He had skipped two grades in elementary school, graduated second in his high school class at sixteen, completed his undergraduate studies with a perfect 4.0 at nineteen, and earned doctoral degrees in anthropology and biology from Harvard by twenty-three.

Second, his book, *Beyond Darwin: The Revolution of the Species*, was an international best seller with more than 100,000 copies in print and another 200,000 digital downloads. The smartly written and beautifully illustrated book not only made the science more interesting and accessible to mainstream readers, it explored several theories that had been mostly ignored by the anthropology community.

One of Adam's most controversial and fascinating theories dealt with the "parallel evolution of prehumans." He had suggested that as many as thirty distinct primate and early human species continued to evolve up until Cro-Magnon, some of which may have been radically unique in appearance due to progenitor primate species, geographic region, climate, food supplies, and environment. He had used genetic modeling and worked with concept artists, 3D illustrators, and CGI animators to show what the various species would have looked like, how and where they would have lived, what they would have hunted and ate, and how they would have socialized.

While many of the parallel species were relatively similar to typical early humans, there were some that were radically different. There was a slow-moving nine-foot-tall, 600 pound primate that was covered with short white fur to the neck but had a hairless face save for a three-inch-long "soul patch" beard under its chin. The species also had thick eyebrows and long head hair. He theorized that the gentle, tree-dwelling vegetarian that would have lived deep in the Amazon jungles may have survived up until approximately 95,000 years ago.

Another evolved primate was a three-foot-tall mandrill-like species that lived in Western Africa 200,000 years ago. They stood almost completely erect and had naturally multicolored faces, with long black hair, wide noses, and long canine teeth. The ferocious pack hunters were highly intelligent, hypersexual, carnivorous, and cannibalistic.

Adam also suggested that there had likely been a "superior" species. These prehumans were taller and thinner than Cro-Magnon with longer necks, arms, and legs. They also possessed a longer cranium that housed a 10 percent larger brain. Already capable of advanced toolmaking and basic farming, this more "elegant" species should have succeeded in addition to, or instead of, Cro-Magnon. However had for some inexplicable reason hit an evolutionary dead end approximately 30,000 years ago. The most logical explanation being that they were not very good fighters.

In addition to the book's original and imaginative premise, sales had been fueled by the publisher's energetic publicist, Samantha "Sammie" Collinsworth. Sammie had gotten feature stories on all the major newspapers and network and cable outlets, as well as appearances on *The Today Show*, the Letterman Show, and several top daytime talk shows.

But Sammie's crowning achievement in pushing Adam out into the pop culture mainstream was getting him named as one of the 50 Hottest Bachelors in America by *People* magazine. He was one of only five noncelebrities featured in the coveted issue, with everyone else being either an actor, musician, or athlete.

While Adam considered his half-page profile a token mention for the eggheads, the handsome and single university professor fit right in.

Standing just a hair over six feet tall with a chiseled face, curly blond hair, deep green eyes, and a radiant smile, the thirty-two-year-old professor looked more like a tennis pro than a serious scientist. It wasn't that great of a stretch however. As a young teen, Adam had been a nationally ranked USTA junior. While he never made the leap to the next level, he still practiced a few times a week and ran four to five miles a day to stay in shape.

Adam's newfound celebrity status had not only powered sales of his book to the Top 10 Nonfiction *New York Times* Best

Seller's List, it brought him an avalanche of fan mail from science geeks, crackpots, and admirers. Female enrollment in his classes tripled, and there was a long waiting list.

*   *   *

"Can't you get this bucket moving any faster?" complained Tamiya Dawes, sitting in the passenger seat beside Adam.

"What do you want, Tam? I've got it floored," he snapped back.

"Six weeks of traipsing around Central America and four days on the road. How much longer?"

"Like I said, we should get there sometime late tomorrow night."

"I am absolutely *dying* to get home," she moaned. "The first thing I want to do is light a vanilla fragrance candle, settle down into a nice hot bubble bath, then curl up in my own bed again."

"Your *own* bed, huh?" he raised an eyebrow.

It was one of the worst-kept secrets on campus that Adam and Tamiya were dating. They'd met at an interdepartmental faculty party eighteen months before. The graduate assistant had come along at the insistence of Professor Frasier Harrington, chair of the Berkeley Genetics Department and her faculty advisor. The rakish, white-haired, sixty-two-year-old professor had a reputation for showing off and occasionally dating his attractive grad students. He had been extremely peeved when Tamiya spent the last two hours of the party talking with Adam. Like a number of his colleagues, Dr. Harrington had already been jealous of the attention the young professor was getting because of that absurd book and the ridiculous fluff piece in *People* magazine. He was further incensed when Adam had essentially monopolized *his* succulent young protégé.

Tamiya sensed the advisor cooling to her not long after she'd started seeing Adam. When she told him that she was going along with Adam on his expedition to Central America, Dr. Harrington had angrily snipped at her. He suggested that she would best be served either interning over the summer or working on her dissertation, questioned her commitment to completing the doctorate program, and wondered aloud if he shouldn't start looking for another graduate assistant.

While her first instinct had been to fire right back at him, she knew it would be tantamount to academic suicide. She'd sucked it up, promising to keep up with her research and writing throughout the summer.

Equally comfortable in tight-fitting, stone-washed jeans or a lab coat, Tamiya had a combination of intelligence, beauty, and a free-spirited nature that set her apart from most of the other grad students. The biracial twenty-five-year-old was the second of three children. A pro football brat, she and her brothers had spent much of their youth moving from football city to football city. Over his thirteen-year career her father, Cedric Dawes, had played linebacker for the Minnesota Vikings, the Chicago Bears, the Kansas City Chiefs, and finally the Tampa Bay Buccaneers. Tamiya's Argentinean mother, Sela, was a former model. She had put her career on hold to stay home with the kids until Cedric retired from football. Afterward she went back to work full-time as an editor for a Spanish-language lifestyle magazine.

While Tamiya had excelled in track and soccer as a child, seeing her father—once the biggest and strongest man she knew—needing to get around with the aid of a cane because of his shot knees had convinced her to follow an academic path. The same couldn't be said for her brothers however. The oldest, Andre, was in his third season with the Vikings but still relegated to the backup cornerback position. Tony, a high-school senior, was an All-Star athlete in football, basketball, and baseball and was being heavily recruited in all three. He also maintained an impressive 3.75 GPA.

Tamiya was a trim, athletically built five-foot-seven beauty with honey-colored skin. While her pert breasts barely filled a C cup, she was confident in the knowledge that she had a fantastic ass. Her beautiful face had a triangular, slightly feline shape, with high cheekbones, large hazel eyes, and soft full lips. She wore her wild mane of long, cinnamon-colored hair in a variety of styles—from the curly shag to dreads. Whenever she needed to look conservative for a meeting or an interview, she'd flat iron it bone straight. While the straight style looked gorgeous on her, most of her friends, including Adam, preferred the sassier untamed look.

"Shhhh," Tamiya hushed him. "The kids'll hear you."

The five college students sitting in the the back of the Winnebago were thoroughly wrung out from the six-week odyssey and, like Tamiya, couldn't wait to get back home.

Twenty-year-old Chance "CJ" Jankovich, a starting player on the top-ranked Cal Bears Berkeley Water Polo team, had taken the class expecting to get an easy A. Instead he'd ended up with an F. Adam had told the tall, muscular young junior that the only way he could bring up the grade was to go along on the expedition and earn fieldwork credit. The coach had backed the professor, telling CJ to "get his butt in gear or get placed on academic suspension."

Shawn "Shaggy" Fitzgerald had gotten his nickname because of his resemblance to the *Scooby Doo* character. The tall, lanky kid had red hair, freckles, oversized ears, and a ragged goatee. Almost always looking like he was either sleepwalking or stoned, the twenty-one-year-old was often at the center of some on-campus demonstration or passing out literature for Greenpeace, Amnesty International, PETA, or any number of activists groups. He was living the college experience to the fullest and in no rush to zip through it. He took the lightest class load possible, and everyone joked that he was on the seven-year program to graduation. It had taken him two years to finish up his freshman year. Shaggy dug the idea of going on a Central America trip in part because he wanted to check out more of the world and in part because he'd heard that the farmers grew potent strains of marijuana. He'd signed up the day Adam posted the trip.

Newton "Newt" Nedry had complained about everything from day 1—the heat, the food, the smells, the insects, the walking, the camping out, the lack of sanitation, the people, and anything else he could think of. Why he had signed up for the expedition in the first place was beyond Adam. Apparently the kid's parents had insisted he go, both to keep him from coming home and playing video games all summer and to hopefully have him lose some weight. The chubby, asthmatic, nineteen-year-old had gotten sick on the trip more times than anyone could count. Twice they had had to wash out the RV because Nedry had thrown up. Even weeks later a faint stench of vomit still lingered in the vehicle. He'd brought along an iPad, an iPhone, and a portable Nintendo handheld game system and was constantly hogging the Winnebago's AC adapters to make sure his electronics always had a full charge.

Standing just under five foot nine, Nedry weighed in at about 220 pounds. Which was twenty pounds less than what he weighed before the trip. He had a fleshy, round face that turned beet-red and drenched with sweat whenever the temperature climbed above eighty-five degrees or he mildly exerted himself. His breathing always sounded labored and wheezing, and at night his snoring kept everyone awake. He had short curly hair and beady brown eyes. At a market in Monte Alban, he bought a wide-brimmed cowboy hat that he'd started wearing to keep the sun out of his eyes or to pull down so that he could ignore his traveling companions.

Twenty-year-old Yeardley Whittle was Adam's top student, and he'd already fast-tracked her to become his graduate assistant next year. Double-majoring in biology and anthropology, she came from a family of intellectuals. Her father was an award-winning chemist, and her mother was a professor at the Harvard School of Medicine. She had been a surprise pregnancy for her then thirty-nine-year-old mother and forty-year-old father, who had thought they were finished with parenthood after their son was born eleven years earlier.

Attractive in a beanpole geeky sort of way, Yeardley never put on makeup and usually wore her mousy brown hair in a ponytail or straight down to cover her ears. She hid her eyes, which were brown with hazel flecks, behind a pair of large, librarian-style glasses.

Unlike the other students who'd brought only T-shirts and jeans, Yeardley looked every bit the part of a young field researcher. She often wore tan or olive-colored khaki shorts, hiking boots with knee-length wool socks, lightweight denim shirts, a multipocketed vest, and a weather-beaten floppy hat. She was a natural at fieldwork and was content to spend hours painstakingly unearthing artifacts or fossils with tiny tools and fine bristle brushes.

Tegan Summers had come on the trip for one reason and one reason only: to get close to Professor Landis. The week after the *People* magazine feature had come out, she had enrolled in his Introduction to Anthropology class, which for the first time ever had filled to capacity and had a waiting list.

The nineteen-year-old golden-blond-haired, sapphire-blue-eyed sophomore had been used to getting what she wanted. As captain of her high school cheerleader squad, Tegan always had males falling all over her, a phenomenon that had been helped tremendously when her parents had sprung for D-cup breast implants for her sixteenth birthday. She had already wrapped her thirty-eight-year-old art history professor around her finger to the point where he was sending her explicit e-mail and text messages that could have both gotten him fired and ended his marriage.

Despite her best efforts at flirting with Adam, however, he had paid her no more attention than any other student. He didn't even seem overly enthusiastic when she'd signed up for the expedition and had instead asked why she as an art major would want to spend all summer on archeological dig sites. She'd made up something about how his class had given her an appreciation of ancient Mayan and Incan art. Somehow the native Californian had expected the expedition would be somewhat akin to the summer trip her senior class had taken to Cancun. She hadn't been prepared for the harsh, third-world conditions; the almost daily afternoon rains; the slogging through rainforests crawling with snakes, lizards, small monkeys, and a bazillion types of insects; or the digging through excavations of old ruins all the time getting leered at by the sweaty, smarmy-looking locals.

Every day they had to work from sunup to sundown. Through it all the professor had treated her like a common student. While she knew he was dating Ms. Dawes, she had figured it wouldn't be much trouble to steal him away. She'd even managed to time it so that he could accidently walked in on her wearing just a thong. She made a halfhearted attempt to cover herself, then gave him an innocent "Oops, but it's okay if you want to come in" smile. He simply apologized and stepped back out of the door.

The entire seduction effort had been a bust.

Sitting in the back of the RV chewing gum, listening to her iPod, and ignoring everyone else, Tegan was wearing a pair of Daisy Dukes, Dior sunglasses, and a boob-hugging, pink T-shirt that read, *Never Underestimate the Power of a Great Set.*

"There it is!" Adam said, pointing to the road sign up ahead. "Redbone exit two miles. I told you we weren't lost."

"Do we really have to stop?" Tamiya complained. "I really just want to get home."

"*Home* is still a day and a half away. So stopping for a half an hour isn't going to make that much of a difference, is it? Anyway we agreed on this."

"I was half asleep at the time. In my normal lucidity I would have never agreed to detouring off to see some crackpot out in the middle of nowhere."

"Look, this guy's been leaving excited voice mails at the office for the last two weeks."

"Riiiight, about his new discovery. Of course it completely slipped his mind to tell you anything of consequence about this supposed new discovery or at least send some kind of photo as proof."

"He's old, Tam."

"No, what he is is another wackjob who read your book and is looking for his fifteen minutes."

"That's the price of fame, babe."

She shook her head with a smile. "No, *babe*, that's the price of you being a sucker and humoring these knuckleheads."

"No, I'm not."

"Really? What about that guy, Clifford, what's his name? He called you last December claiming to have found a Sasquatch burial ground, didn't he? He even sent you that skullcap as proof. And what happened? You wasted nearly two weeks DNA testing and carbon dating the thing before you finally figured out it was an irradiated orangutan skull with a bad dye job. And don't even start me on that little Area 51 alien."

Holding up his hands in surrender, Adam said, "Okay, okay."

"Face it, handsome, you're just a sucker for these things, and all the crackpots know it."

"Well, whatever, I'm taking the exit."

"Fine," she relented. "But don't think I'm agreeing because I think this makes a bit of sense or because I can't resist to those sexy green eyes of yours. I'm letting you go because the kids could use a break."

The Winnebago exited off the highway onto the unpaved exit road, kicking up a swirling plume of dust and small bits of gravel in its wake.

When they came to the end of the exit, they were greeted by a rusted and bent stop sign. The narrow, two-lane dusty road stretched endlessly in both directions.

They had no idea which way to go.

On the other side of the road was a rundown, two-pump service station. From the circular signs and some of the painted-over raised lettering, it was obvious that the station had once been a Texaco. However at some point it had been repainted a dark-blue and given the new brand identity of Mel's Gasoline & Service. The paint had faded and chipped from age, dust, and the arid climate, and a piece of red Texaco star could be seen peeking out from underneath the paint on the main sign. Only one of the old dial-type gas pumps was working. The other had a yellow "out of service" bag pulled over the nozzle.

As soon as they pulled into the station, the rear passenger door swung open and Nedry hopped out. Tegan came out a second later chasing him.

"Ladies first, Nerdly!" she screamed.

"I gotta pee," the lumbering young man called back, not breaking stride. He had correctly figured that the station would only have one restroom, and he wasn't going to wait. The toilet in the RV had stopped working three days ago.

"So do I, jerk!"

Adam, Tamiya, and the other students emerged from the RV stretching their arms and legs, which felt good after hours of being folded up in the constricted area.

A young man came out from the garage bay, wiping down his hands on a rag that was stained with large splotches of black grease. He wore a pair of oil-stained, light-blue service station coveralls. The name "Billy" was embroidered on the oval patch on his breast pocket.

Twenty-year-old Billy Lightfoot was half-breed Navajo. Standing just under six feet tall with the lean, well-muscled physique of an athlete, he could have easily passed for a male model. His masculine sculpted face was embellished with high cheekbones and a strong jawline. His sky-blue eyes contrasted against his copper-colored skin and shoulder-length raven-black hair.

"Help you, folks?" Billy asked as he walked up.

"I need to fill it up," replied Adam.

Billy pointed to the pump dial that read in neat delineated rows: 9-9-.-9-7/8. The dial was stuck between the 7 and the 8.

"Dial's been broke for weeks, I'd have ta guestimate."

"That's not a problem."

"Okay." Billy pulled the nozzle out of the pump holster and started filling the RV's tank. As the gas flowed he counted silently to himself in a cadence that suggested he was marking off the gallons.

Adam had started unfolding a roadmap. "We're trying to find this place, and it's not coming up on my GPS."

"This is Redbone, man. Population like 270. We don't show up on no GPS."

Nedry had come back out of the filthy restroom, went around to the rear of the Winnebago, and opened up the large cooler to fish out a can of Coke.

"Well, maybe you can help me," Adam said. "I'm looking for a person who's supposed to live around here . . . a Mr. Joseph Cunninghan?"

"Loco Joe?" Billy laughed. "Ye-up, his place is 'bout six miles up the road that way. You go up about five more miles, then turn left onto the dirt road. He's got an old sign out there pointing to his place, ya can't miss it."

Adam folded up the map. "Great, thanks."

Tamiya came up behind Adam and put her hand on his shoulder. A big, impish smile sliced across her face. "Lo-co Joe," she said. "You do know how to pick 'em, babe."

Either not wanting to or not being able to hold it while others took turns in the dingy station restroom, Shaggy had walked back from relieving himself on the other side of the station.

He spotted a vehicle just inside the garage bay. "Whoa killer bike, dude!" he exclaimed.

"It's mine," Billy called back.

The fully customized 450 cc Honda gleamed with a black, red, and blue paintjob and had the stylized name *Renegade* incorporated into the graphic design. A matching helmet dangled by a strap from the handlebar.

Shaggy was crouched down on his haunches admiringly gliding his hand along the machine. "This baby looks like one of them X Games bikes."

"Yeah, me and some of my buds fool around."

"How fast'll she do? A hundred twenty, hundred thirty?"

"Somethin' like that."

"Cool."

Billy had finished filling up the RV. He had counted out thirty gallons.

"Okay, that'll be a hundred and twenty-two bucks," he said.

Adam pulled out his wallet and counted out the cash.

By then all of the students had gotten back to the Winnebago and were picking through the snacks and sodas.

As Yeardley was taking a drink from a cold bottle of Sprite, she looked out into the long stretch of desert beyond the station. "Who's that?" she asked.

Sitting cross-legged in a clearing about fifty yards away was an old Navajo. The ninety-two-year-old man's ancient face was a roadmap of wrinkles and experience. He had long white hair and smoke-gray eyes. He was clothed in the attire of a Navajo

Hataalii—a light-blue shirt with bone breastplate, buckskin pants, a handwoven white poncho with elaborate designs and patterns, fringed deerskin moccasin boots, and turquoise beads. He wore a colorful and elaborate headdress of porcupine quills and eagle feathers. In his hands he was holding two traditional spirit rattles. Eyes closed, he was rhythmically chanting and shaking the rattles.

Seeing the man, a look of "what the f—" crossed Billy's face.

"It's an old Indian dude," Shaggy said.

Billy yelled out to the man, "Hey, you old fool! How many times I gotta tell you to get out of here?"

The old man just continued chanting and shaking the spirit sticks.

"All you're doin' is perpetuating stereotypes, you know!"

"Who is he?" asked Tamiya asked.

"A nobody," Billy said. Then almost as a minor footnote, he added, "Just my crazy ole fool of an uncle."

"Your uncle?" Yeardley asked.

"Great-great-uncle actually."

They watched as the old man went about his ritual.

"Is that Navajo he's chanting in?" Adam wondered out loud.

"Ye-up," Billy confirmed.

"Do you know what he's saying?"

"Same thing he's been yappin' 'bout for a couple of months now: he saying, 'The demons have returned to the mountain'."

3

Loco Joe Cunningham's place was exactly where Billy had directed them. Built on a dusty patch of land devoid of any greenery, the dilapidated three-room cabin had originally been constructed in the 1930s. The wooden shack was weathered to a desiccated gray and, over the years, had been patched up with two-by-fours, plywood, sheet metal, or whatever other material was handy to hold the structure together.

Loco Joe had been a fixture in the area for more than forty years. At one point he'd even unsuccessfully run for mayor of the small town. A jack-of-all-trades, the old man scratched out a living as a prospector, collector, tinkerer, taxidermist, and peddler.

Wearing a pair of striped dungarees held up by fraying suspenders, a dingy white T-shirt that was sweat-stained at the armpits, a pair of worn and cracked cowboy boots, and a tattered cap perched atop on his head, he looked every bit the part of the town eccentric. The scarecrow-thin, seventy-one-year-old had bulbous eyes framed by thick white brows, wrinkled skin, thinning gray-white hair, and four days of stubbly beard growth on his pointed chin. Something about the man reminded Adam of a rooster.

Loco Joe stood behind the battered screen door suspiciously eyeing the young visitors. Then his eyebrows rose in recognition. "Dr. Landis?" he asked, "Dr. Adam Landis?"

"Yes, I am," Adam confirmed.

The door swung open, and the man broke into a broad smile that revealed several rotted and missing teeth. "Well, I'll be," he exclaimed. "I never expected you to come all the way out here." He took Adam's hand in both of his and began vigorously shaking it.

"It was on the way."

"And here I thought you were just payin' this ole fool lip service."

"I couldn't exactly ignore all the voice mails you left at my office. You sounded pretty excited about your find."

"Well, you ain't gonna regret it, I guarantee you." He ushered Adam into the humble shack, beckoning the students to follow. "C'mon in, c'mon in."

"Can't some of us just wait in the truck?" Nedry asked, his portable game player already in hand.

"No," Adam replied. "Consider this part of your educational requirement."

"An education on what?" Tegan remarked, turning up her nose so as not to have to breathe in the stale, organic stench of the shack. From the body odor the old man was emanating, she wondered how long it had been since he'd even seen a bar of soap.

"Oh, this is gonna be educational. You ain't never seent nothin' like this, young lady. Heck, I ain't never seent nothin' like it, and I been on this planet a far cry longer than you."

"Mr. Cunningham," Adam cut in.

"Call me Joe. Old Joe, Crazy Joe, whatevers you want."

"How about Loco Joe?" Tamiya said wryly.

Adam narrowed his eyes at her with a disapproving scowl. "Unfortunately, Joe, we don't have much time. If you could just show me where—"

"Here, I got it right out back."

Loco Joe hobbled with a stiff-kneed limp that favored his right leg. The old man led them out the back screen door.

"It was Lucille what actually spotted him," Loco Joe explained. He patted the snout of a old burro that was corralled within a small split-rail fence that ran off the shack.

Lucille's matted down fur was the color of chocolate pudding. She was using her tail to swat flies.

Adam looked into the broken-down burro's huge brown eyes. "We'll have to remember to give her some credit if this discovery of yours makes into my next book."

This got an excited chuckle out of the old man.

He led them in the direction of a rusted storage shed. Looking as if it could fall down at any moment, the twenty-foot-by-twenty-foot shed was even more battered than the cabin. Boards were askew in a several places, and the tin roof had a large hole where it had rusted through.

Tamiya came up behind Adam and playfully whispered in his ear, "And they were never heard from again."

Just then, two vicious pit bulls tore out from behind the storage shed. Barking loudly and charging wildly toward the students, they looked like hounds from hell. The dog on the left was dirty-gray with an irregularly shaped white spot on its face. The one on the right was mud-brown in color. Their dark eyes filled with murderous intent, drool slinging from their sharp-toothed snapping jaws, the pit bulls closed in on the terrified group.

Adam put his arms out, protectively pushing the students and Tamiya back behind him.

Reaching the ends of their heavy chains, both dogs were yanked to a twisting and sudden stop less than three feet away from the students.

"Don't worry, don't worry," Loco Joe reassured as he grabbed up a length of both chains in his hands. The dogs started calming down and began wagging their stump tails. "Their bark is much worse than their bite."

"Well, their bark is pretty damned bad," said a still rattled Shaggy. "Now I gotta go check my underwear."

"My babies just get excited 'bout meetin' new folk." He swatted the dogs on the hindquarters, shooing them away. "Now go on git outta here, you two!"

The dogs raced off and disappeared back behind the shed.

Although the shed looked as if a strong wind could topple it, Loco Joe had nevertheless taken the precaution of padlocking the door.

With a creak, the rickety door opened into the nearly pitch-black room. It hadn't been evident from the outside that the shutters covering the two windows had long been nailed shut. The only illumination came from the narrow shaft of light that beamed down through the hole in the roof.

An almost overwhelming stench of formaldehyde immediately wafted out through the open door.

"Uggh, what is that stink?" Tegan complained, her pert, sensitive nose picking up on the smell a half second before the others.

"Oh, that'd be the formaldehyde," Loco Joe said.

"Formaldehyde?" Adam asked.

"God, it smells like a friggin' morgue or something," Nedry said, cupping his hand over his nose and mouth.

Loco Joe continued leading them. "C'mon now, it's right in here."

Nedry took a quick step back. "Are you crazy? I ain't goin' in there!"

The old man disappeared into the darkened room. There was the sound of fumbling around and clanging metal.

"I say we cut out now," Shaggy suggested. "Dude's probably an axe murderer."

"Shawn," Adam warned.

"Here's that light," came the old man's voice as he tugged on the pull string.

There was a click, and the yellowing forty-watt bulb came to life, barely filling the shed interior with light.

"Jeezus!" CJ cried.

Less than a foot away from the student's face was a huge barn owl; its soft wings were spread wide and its clawed talons open and ready to strike.

Loco Joe playfully pushed the stuffed owl to the side. It swung back and forth on a long string. "Now don't you worry yerself, son, that old bird's been stuffed fer years."

"You could warn a guy," the young man grumbled.

Adam and the students took a good look around the room. In addition to rusted farming tools, prospecting equipment, kerosene lanterns, lengths of old rope, wheelbarrows, buckets and burlap sacks, there were scores of dead and meticulously preserved animals. Deer, rabbits, birds, coyotes, snakes, prairie dogs, bobcats—all frozen in poses that echoed how they appeared in life.

"Eww," Tegan complained. "These dead things are disgusting."

"Tegan, cut it out," Yeardley was annoyed by the drama queen's attitude.

"I tolt y'all I did some taxidermy. We got a bunch o' hunters in town. I just finished that one for—"

"Joe," Adam said impatiently, "we're short on time."

"Yes-sirree. It's right over here."

The old man stepped over the assorted debris covering the floor and went over to what looked to be a large object that was draped over by a heavy dirt-stained fabric tarp.

Loco Joe grabbed one end of the tarp and yanked. "Now y'all take a look at this," he announced.

The tarp slid away, revealing a transparent five-foot-high-by-thirty-inch diameter glass cylinder. The tank looked like it could have come right out of Frankenstein's laboratory. Inside, a small, human-shaped figure was floating in a yellowish-brown-tinged solution of formaldehyde.

Nedry jumped back. "Jeezus! He's got a dead kid in there!"

Tegan screamed.

"Dude *is* a friggin' axe murderer!" Shaggy exclaimed.

The students were backing toward the door.

"Wait, *wait*, wait!" Adam ordered.

Everyone froze.

Adam leaned in closer, peering into the hermetically sealed vat. "It's . . . not human."

"See, I tolt ya," Loco Joe exclaimed proudly.

"What do you mean 'not human'? Tamiya asked. She and the students were still shaken by the macabre revelation. They nervously inched forward.

"I mean just that. It's not human."

"Then what the hell is it?"

"I was hoping the perfessor'd tell me," Loco Joe said.

Adam leaned in close and peered into the glass-walled canister.

The three-foot-tall creature was curled up in semifetal position. Its clawed hands were under its chin as if in prayer. Instead of skin it was covered in thousands of brownish snakelike scales. However, strangely enough, it had dark tendril-like hair on what remained of its head. The carcass had been badly damaged by the scavengers. Much of the face had been torn and eaten away; the back had been stripped down, exposing several picked-clean ribs. There was a huge chunk out of the torso, and there were several deep bites in the legs. Strands of ragged flesh and entrails floated in the liquid.

"Where did it come from?" Adam asked the old man curiously.

"Like I said, me and Lucille fount it out in the desert a couple o' weeks ago. At first we thought it was just regular road kill that had been dead for a while 'cuz the buzzards had already got to it pretty good. But then when we got closer, we thought it looked like it mighta been a person, so I fired off a couple of rounds to scare them nasty scavengers away. Then I runs up and that's when I saw it. I knew right then and there it weren't no human.

"When I got it back here I tried to preserve it as best I could until I could show it to somebody who could figure it out. Good thing I keep a stock of formaldehyde for my taxidermy business."

"Good thing," Adam complimented. "You did a good job, considering."

Although the formaldehyde had arrested the decomposition process, Adam knew it wasn't ideal. "I'm going to need to take a better look at it, Joe. First let me see if I can figure out some preliminary typing for this guy. Can I take it out of here?"

"Yes-sirree," Loco Joe said enthusiastically. "Lemme get a screwdriver over here and I can pop the top."

Loco Joe hobbled off to his workbench.

"What are you doing?" Tamiya hissed through her teeth.

"I need to take a look at it," said Adam.

"That old man is crazy! God only knows why he cobbled this sideshow freak thing together."

"I don't think it's . . ."

"Here we go," announced Loco Joe as he hobbled back over with the foot-long flathead screwdriver.

The old man slid the screwdriver's blade between the top of the glass and the hard plastic lid. He wiggled it back and forth to work it in, and then with a twist of his wrist, the top separated with a vacuum hiss.

The odor of freshly released formaldehyde vapors filled the room. However the students' complaints were restricted to exaggerated facial expressions.

"Joe, we're going to have to take it out of the solution so I can examine it more closely," Adam said.

He spotted Loco Joe's taxidermy worktable, which was already covered with a clear plastic lining. "That's perfect. Can we use that?"

"Yes, sir."

"All right, help me get it out of here?"

Adam pushed up his shirt sleeves, plunged his bare arm into the formaldehyde, and hooked a hand under the creature's armpit. This extracted winces and groans of disgust from a couple of the students.

Tamiya just shook her head as she watched. Adam had a determined schoolboy expression on his face, like first grader digging into a cookie jar.

"Careful, careful," Loco Joe said as he lent a hand maneuvering the creature for Adam to get a better purchase.

"That is completely gross," sneered Tegan.

Yeardley stepped forward to assist Adam and the old man. Together, the three pulled the dripping thirty-pound carcass completely out of the container and carried it over to the worktable.

After setting it down on the plastic tarp, Adam rolled the carcass onto its back and pulled the stiff limbs into a spread eagle position. Each tug and twist was accompanied by wet, sticky, cracking sounds.

"That is one ugly critter," Shaggy commented with a somewhat uneasy laugh.

Adam held up a silencing hand to his students. He needed to concentrate. He had never seen anything like this. The creature clearly had a humanlike morphology but appeared almost like a reptilian mammalian hybrid. Its scaly skin was a dark tan in color with a subtle stripe pattern. The underside chest area was a lighter color and was mottled with brownish spots. Its remaining arm was thin and slightly longer than a comparably sized human arm. Each clawed hand had three long fingers with an opposable thumb. Its lower legs also appeared to be constructed different from a human's. Its four-toed feet seemed to be designed for grasping and climbing like that of a tree-dwelling primate.

Only about half of the creature's face remained intact. Using what was there, and his knowledge of forensic anthropology, Adam could extrapolate in his mind how the face would have appeared.

"It probably looked like a little demon when it was alive," he muttered mostly to himself.

Using his thumb, Adam pulled up one of the lids to reveal a bright yellow iris that was glazed over in a death stare. Instead of being round, the pupil was slit shaped like a reptile's.

"That's strange."

He methodically continued his examination for several minutes, occasionally making remarks intended for no one in particular as he was oblivious to everyone else around him. Using his thumb and index finger, he squeezed one of the swollen wounds, and a thick bluish-green pus oozed out.

"Can you at least put on some gloves or something?" Tamiya asked.

"I doubt our friend has a pair of surgical gloves lying around here."

Loco Joe shook his head, "Nope, just my work gloves."

"I have some," Yeardley volunteered. "I also have a specimen collection kit."

Yeardley took off her backpack and set it on the ground. She rummaged around and located a pair of thin latex gloves and small black case that contained several stainless steel precision instruments. The tweezers, scalpels, scissors, picks, syringes, collection bottles, and other tools were lined in indented storage slots. She handed the gloves and case to Adam.

"Thank you, Yeardley," he complimented.

For several minutes, Adam poked and prodded around with the instruments. His tongue was fixed slightly askew in his mouth, like a ten-year-old with his first junior scientist kit. He took out one of the syringes and extracted some of the pus. He plunged the other syringe deep into the dead creature's chest and withdrew a clear fluid. He capped off both syringes and placed them back into their slots in the case.

There was a wet, sticky sound as he rolled the carcass onto its side. He could see that the creature's back had been almost completely stripped to the bone.

"Tam, come take a look," he said, excitedly.

"No, thank you," she declined emphatically.

"Stop acting like a baby and come here. You're a scientist."

"You an anthropologist too, missy?" Loco Joe asked.

"Geneticist," Tamiya corrected.

"And a good one," Adam added.

Tamiya sighed deeply and then reluctantly went over and stood beside Adam. The curious students crowded in closer to get a better look.

Adam took one of the instruments and pulled back a flap of ragged flesh. Hard grayish white bones could be seen beneath the thick purple muscle tissue and tangle of veins. "Take a look at this skeletal structure," he said. "It's similar to ours, but it has two extra ribs. And see these bones protruding out here? There may have been an extra set of limbs here, I'm not sure. And I haven't even started trying to get to the organs. What do you think?"

For several minutes, Tamiya closely and silently examined the carcass.

"Well?" Adam asked impatiently.

She held up a silencing hand.

"Well," he asked again.

"Well," Tamiya started, still not looking up, "it's not a cataloged species. It's neither a primate nor is it reptilian. Best guess would be some kind of hybrid."

"*So* what do you think it is?"

"Honestly?"

"Yes, honestly."

"A hoax."

"Ain't no hoax," Loco Joe exclaimed defensively.

Tamiya gave the old man a sarcastic grin. "Of course it is," she said. "This is something that has been stitched together from God knows what. Look around this zoo."

"I said I do taxidermy."

"And so you grab a piece of this animal and a piece of that one and put together this little Frankenstein's monster here."

Loco Joe protested, "This is exactly how I fount it! Exactly!"

"I don't know, Tam," Adam said. "I'm not seeing any suture marks."

"That's because he probably stuck it out in the desert for a day or two to let the scavengers and elements rough it up enough to cover any handiwork and make it look convincing."

"No, I didn't," Loco Joe repeated.

"Look, I know you dig this kind of thing, handsome, but you need to be realistic. You're a trained anthropologist, and you know damned well there is no precedent anywhere for a creature like this. Nothing related. No evolutionary path even close. This is obviously something this guy dreamed up and cooked up. He was probably planning to sell it to some circus sideshow. That was until of course you come along."

"You can call me gullible all you want, Tam, but I'm gonna have to disagree with you on this one. I mean this is far too sophisticated to be something he slapped together from unrelated parts. Everything fits perfectly. There are no surgical incisions, no stitches, nothing to suggest that this isn't a viable animal life form."

"That's exactly what I said," agreed Loco Joe. "I think."

Adam turned to the old man. "Of course, I can't verify anything just based upon a preliminary examination, Joe. I have to get this specimen into a lab."

"What do you mean?"

"There are a whole battery of tests I'd have to run—a complete pathology workup, DNA analyses, chemical analyses of the body fluids, facial reconstruction, imaging, precise measurements, everything. If this is the 'real McCoy' so to speak, I have to find out exactly what it is, what species it may be related to, how it evolved, and how it could have gotten out in the desert where you found it in the first place."

Tamiya looked at Adam incredulously. "You cannot be serious."

"You can say you 'told me so' later, Tam," he said almost dismissively then remembered to tag on a boyish smile, to which she rolled her eyes.

"So, Joe, how does that sound?"

A look of confusion crossed the old man's face. "A lab?"

"Berkeley has one of the most advanced research facilities in the country. We'll be able to run practically any test imaginable. Then we can figure out exactly what you have here, sir. The evidence would be irrefutable."

"Well, I was kinda hopin' you'd be able to tell me straight out."

Adam laughed somewhat uncomfortably. "That would be impossible, Joe."

"Cain't ya just write me up a letter to confirm that it's a new species?"

"Not without thorough testing and analysis."

"Well, I weren't really planning on just lettin' it go. I mean, that little guy could be worth a lot of money."

Tamiya suddenly perked up. A wry skeptical smile crossing her lips. "Of course, it could," she said playfully nodding her head in agreement. She knew what Loco Joe was up to.

"Joe, I can promise you that if this discovery of yours is genuine, the university would be willing to buy it from you," Adam said.

"And they'd pay more than the sideshow," Tamiya added.

Adam glowered at her.

"I don't know," Joe said.

"How about if *I* just buy it from you right now?" Adam suggested. He went into his wallet thumbing through bills and traveler's checks. "I can pay you . . . twenty-five hundred in cash and traveler's checks now and another, let's say, twenty-five when I get back day after tomorrow. That's five thousand all together."

"Are you completely out of your mind!" Tamiya cried. At the most she figured her boyfriend would offer the old man a couple of hundred dollars for the freak show.

Adam ignored her. "How about it, Joe?"

"Five thousand dollars a lot o' money," the old man said. "But I cain't sell it. This could be a major discover, maybe even worth a million dollars."

"Sure it can," Tamiya drawled.

A look of dejection crossed Adam's face.

But then Loco Joe's face lit up as he hit upon an idea. "But I could *rent* it to ya fer that amount."

"Rent it?"

Tamiya rolled her eyes. "Oh for god's sake."

"Sure thing. You can write me up a little rental contract on your school letterhead. And if this little guy turns out to be a major discovery, well then, I wouldn't be out my million dollars."

Tamiya shot the old man a glare. "And what if it turns out to be crap? Do we get a refund?"

"It ain't—"

Adam jumped in, "I'm willing to take that gamble."

Tamiya resisted the urge to grab Adam by the throat and smack him back to his senses. But it wasn't the first time she'd seen him duped by one of these crackpots, and she figured it wouldn't be the last.

Fifteen minutes later, Adam, CJ, and Shaggy had zipped the rancid dripping carcass up in a jumbo-sized transparent specimen bag and carted it out to the Winnebago. Adam had them empty the large cooler of snacks and drinks, leaving only the ice.

As the men hoisted the ziploclike bag into the cooler, Tegan's face turned a sickly green. "Remind me to never eat anything that comes out of there again."

4

"Do you have *any* idea where you are?" Tamiya asked.

"Ummm, not really," Adam reluctantly admitted.

It had gone from dusk to virtually pitch-black within minutes of their leaving Loco Joe's place. Somewhere along the way, Adam had taken a wrong turn, and they'd spent the past forty-five minutes driving around in circles. Adam had been quietly hoping that if he just kept driving around, a recognizable road would pop up on the portable GPS.

The students were in the back absorbed in their own worlds. Most were listening to music or watching movies on their portable players. Shaggy had dozed off. The ever-conscientious Yeardley was on her tablet, typing in notes about the new specimen.

The RV was creeping along at just under twenty miles an hour.

"I figured as much," Tamiya concluded. "Since I'm pretty sure this is the third time we've passed this area."

"I can't see any landmarks to navigate by."

"That's because it's pitch-black out here. We should have left Loco Joko's when it was still light. But no, you had to get your little dead monster."

"Are you done?"

"For the moment. So what do we do now?"

Before he could answer, something zipped past the RV on the passenger side. It looked and felt like a fast-moving shadow.

"What the heck was that!" asked a startled Tamiya.

"What was what?"

Another shadow zipped by, this time on the driver's side. Adam reflexively took his foot off the gas.

"Okay," he said. "That I saw."

"Hey, there's another one!" CJ called up as he looked out the back window. A dark blob seemed to leap from one side of the road to the other.

"Something's definitely after us, man!" Shaggy had been startled awake.

Looking around frantically, the students were able to make out several of the fast-moving blobs. Some were right behind them; others were moving along the canyon walls above.

"What the hell are they!?" Adam asked aloud. He was straining his eyes and looking around, trying to get a better angle.

"Whatever they are, they're closing in," CJ said nervously.

Adam pressed his foot on the gas, flooring it. The Winnebago began picking up speed as it spewed desert sand and dirt from its spinning tires. The RV's headlight beams bounced around erratically as the vehicle rolled over rocks and uneven desert terrain.

Two more shadows zipped by. They seemed to be emitting a whirring sound, but it was mostly drowned out by the sound of the RV's diesel-powered engine.

"You gotta get us outta here, Professor Landis!" Nedry cried.

"I'm trying!" Adam yelled back.

"What do they want!?" Tegan cried.

A blob knocked up against the right side of the Winnebago, sending a thumping sound through the passenger compartment.

Tegan and Nedry both cried out.

Frantically, Adam turned the wheel in the opposite direction and sent the vehicle in an uncontrolled fishtail spin. Unable to find purchase in the fine desert sand, the RV did a complete 360 degree spin, then another, and finally spun another half revolution before coming to a stop. The engine cut, and everything went dark.

"Dammit!" Adam pounded the dashboard in frustration.

He turned the key, but the starter only whinnied like a sickly horse. He tried again. Again the engine whinnied but even weaker the second time.

The terrified students were frantically looking out of the windows into the utter blackness, anticipating another attack.

Adam vigorously pumped the gas pedal several times in succession, the squeaking and flapping of the mechanism attesting to his panic. "C'mon! C'mon!"

"Adam!" Tamiya cried.

He turned the key again, and the RV sprung back to life.

"Thank god!" Tamiya exhaled.

Adam shifted into drive and slammed his foot on the gas. However, the vehicle didn't move forward.

The tires spun furiously but were unable to find traction. He shifted into reverse, engaging the other set of wheels, but the results were the same. He tried shifting into forward and reverse several more times, flooring the gas pedal, but the vehicle wouldn't grab into the loose sand.

"Dammit! We must have spun out into a dune or something." Adam determined. "We're stuck."

"What do we do?" Tamiya asked.

"What about whatever it is that's out there?" Shaggy reminded.

As if on cue, a number of bright lights suddenly switched on all around them.

The professor and students were baffled and mystified by the sudden appearance of sixteen cones of light encircling the vehicle.

"What the hell?" stated Adam.

CJ looked to the left, right, and behind. "They're all around us."

"*Who's* all around us?" asked a nervous Nedry.

"And what do they want?" added Yeardley.

"Out here, probably some inbred mutants looking to wear our skins as coats," Shaggy suggested only half kidding.

"Shut up," snapped Tegan.

"All right, everybody quiet and calm down," said Adam.

Realizing they were trapped and unable to move, he turned off the RV.

"What are you doing?" Tamiya demanded.

"We're not going anywhere," replied Adam.

"But we have no idea who's out there."

"I'm not gonna find out staying in here, am I?"

"Let's just keep the doors locked and call 911."

"We barely get signal. And even if we *could* reach someone, how long would it take them to get here?"

He put his hand on the inside door handle.

Tamiya grabbed his arm. "You're not actually going *out* there!"

"Do you have a better idea?"

"You want me to come with you, professor?" CJ asked, his hand already on the door handle.

"No. Stay here."

Adam popped open the door and set one foot on the ground. Before getting completely out, he took a quick look at the back wheel and confirmed his assessment of being stuck fast. There was no way to drive out.

"Be careful, teach," Shaggy called out.

Adam stepped out into the darkness. Out of the corner of his eye, he could see the frightened faces of his students and Tamiya illuminated by the circle of lights. Nedry's face was pressed against one of the windows, and he was hyperventilating so hard it was fogging up the glass.

Adam looked out into the darkness at the conical beams that sliced through from all directions. Bathed in the glow, he knew that whoever or whatever was on the other side could easily see him, but even holding up a hand to partially shield his eyes, he wasn't able to make them out.

A man-shaped silhouette moved into the light directly in front of him.

"You lost, man?" The vaguely familiar voice was both asking a question and stating a fact.

As he stepped forward into the light, a broad smile formed on Billy Lightfoot's face. Several other young men stepped forward into the lights being emitted from their motorcycle headlights.

The Renegades were local teens who were into motocross bike racing. The sixteen all-male members ranged in age from fifteen to twenty-one years and were a mix of seven Navajos, three Apaches, two half breeds, one Mexican-American, and three whites. Billy was both the best rider and cofounder of the group.

Adam didn't know whether to be relieved or furious at seeing the young gas station attendant.

Tamiya didn't have that dilemma. She immediately jumped out of the passenger side of the RV and stormed up beside Adam. "What kind of stupid games are you idiots playing!?" she demanded.

Billy held up his hands, stepping backward. "Whoa, whoa, whoa soul sista. We was just trying to get your attention."

"How? By riding around with your lights off and playing chicken with a four-ton vehicle? You're damned lucky we didn't run one of you fools over."

"My bros and I was out doing some night ridin'."

"Night riding?" Adam asked.

"Yep, we ride by moonlight when it's full like this." Billy tilted his chin up in the direction of the swollen moon. "We keep our lights off and engines muffled so the law don't come and chase us off. We was up on that ridge 'bout a quarter mile away and seen your truck driving around in circles. Tourists tend to get turned 'round on these roads at night. There's a dead end about two hundred more yards up in that direction. That little protection gate they got down there's been broke since winter. You drive through that and it's a fifty foot drop straight down."

Tamiya regarded the young man suspiciously. "Well . . . thanks for that. But you still scared the hell out of us."

Her words might have carried a little more impact had Shaggy not taken that moment to start rapping on the glass.

He popped open the window and stuck his head out, "Awesome bikes, dudes!" he said, grinning ear to ear and giving them a thumbs up.

Adam stepped forward. "So, now that we know you're not trying to waylay us, do you think some of you can help us push our RV out of this sand trap and then point us in the right direction?"

"Sure, man," Billy agreed.

A few minutes later Billy and several of his friends, along with Shaggy and CJ, had managed to push the Winnebago out of the dune and back onto the dirt road. Billy even took a quick look at the engine to make sure it was running okay and hadn't gotten sand inside.

"How far away is that town?" Adam asked after Billy put down the hood.

"Redbone? 'Bout four miles give or take."

"Is there a hotel in town?"

Billy laughed. "Man, this is friggin' Redbone. The Ritz closed down years ago."

"A motel or inn then? Someplace we can stay for the night."

"What!?" Tamiya protested.

"It's already past nine, Tam. We can check in somewhere, stay the night, and get back on the road first thing."

She exhaled a scoff.

"We can lead ya there if you wants," Billy said. "Make sure you don't get lost again."

"We'd appreciate it."

"It'll only cost ya a hundred."

5

Founded in 1881 and with a population of 263, Redbone, Arizona, was one of those small desert towns that appeared to spring up out of nowhere and continued to exist with no visible means of support.

Its citizens were a mix of farmers, small ranchers, long haul truckers, plant workers, and retirees. Approximately one-fifth of its residents commuted an hour or so to jobs at manufacturing plants, mining operations, or other industries in larger towns or cities. The few shops in town included a general store/post office, a sport-and-game store, a barbershop, a hardware store, a diner, and an inn. There was a bare-bones town government that consisted of a part-time mayor, a three-man sheriff's department, and a volunteer fire department. While some of the children in town were homeschooled, seventeen kids and teens boarded the old school bus every morning at 6:30 AM for the forty-one-mile, fifty-five-minute ride to Carson Flats Elementary School and Carson Flats High School.

The town itself consisted of only a handful of commercial establishments and two small municipal buildings. The surrounding houses were a hodgepodge of clapboards, simple ramblers, mobile homes, and trailers.

In the early 1950s the town had briefly become something of a minor tourist attraction when Earl Carpenter, the ironically named local handyman, came up with the idea of building a twenty-five-foot-long shovel. He had charged tourists a quarter a head to see the World's Largest Shovel, which he kept in his back yard. The next year, he built an accompanying twenty-five-foot-tall pickax, and upped the fee to forty cents.

In hopes of generating tourism and getting the town on the map, the mayor at the time, Franklin C. Andrews, Jr. bought the set for seventy-five dollars. The shovel and axe were set up on a small cement slab just in front of the city hall office. A week later they put up three signs on the highway, "See the World's Largest Shovel and Pickax twenty miles ahead," "Don't Miss the World's Largest Shovel and Pickax five miles ahead," and "the World's Largest Shovel and Pickax, next exit."

In the first year alone Mayor Andrews had estimated that the attraction bought in at least two hundred tourists. Every once in a while he'd look out his window to see an unfamiliar face or family of faces craning their heads up in awe as they took in the pair of massive tools. Most everyone took photos of family members posed in front of the display. Finally, Redbone was going to be known for something.

The mayor had been in the planning stages of commissioning two additional pieces for the collection,—a hammer and a screwdriver, when he'd gotten the official looking *cease and desist* letter that was postmarked from Austria. It seemed that a small town in that country had been promoting a collection of giant tools, cups, books, shoes, glasses, and other everyday pieces for nearly a decade. Because the giant-sized objects were on a slightly larger scale than the shovel and pickax in Redbone, the town had no right to call theirs the "world's largest." Although Andrews briefly toyed with the idea of changing the signs to "World's Second Largest Shovel and Pickax" or "America's Largest Shovel and Pickax," he worried that another official letter might arrive to challenge one of those claims, and the town coffers could certainly not afford a lawsuit. In the end, they had repainted the signs to read, "Giant Shovel and Pickax," which did not have nearly the same draw as "world's largest."

Over time the neglected highway signs fell down, rusted and crumbled into the desert. The giant pickax succumbed to rust and termite infestation in the mid-1980s. The shovel, however, managed to hang on and remained on display.

Led by an escort of nine motorcycles, the Winnebago drove past the welcome sign and into the town of Redbone at ten minutes to ten o'clock. The ruckus of the motocross bikes and an unfamiliar vehicle pulling into town was probably the most excitement of the day. Adam noticed a number of lights come on in houses as the convoy approached.

Billy pulled up beside the RV and motioned to Adam to roll down the window.

"Here ya go, safe and sound," the young half-breed said.

The bikes all slowed to a stop in perfect synchronization as the RV continued on into town. Out of his rearview mirror, Adam could see the transition to red taillights as the bikes turned around and headed in the opposite direction back out of town.

Although it was dark, Adam could tell that even in the day, the town itself wouldn't be much to look at. There were small weather-beaten homes—most of which were hand constructed of wood or brick. Mobile homes sat on tiny plots of land, rooted to the ground or propped up on cinderblocks and no longer mobile. There was a municipal building at the center of town that for some reason had a giant shovel out front.

They headed in the direction of the inn.

* * *

The Redbone Inn was a long single-story cinderblock-and-siding building. It was gray with green trim and a green metal roof. A weather-beaten oval sign hung on rusted chains out front. The inn consisted of eight guest rooms with a manager's residence and office anchoring the front end. The rooms were sequentially numbered 101-108 although 1-8 would have sufficed.

Each room had two full-sized beds made up with sparse clothing and a thick, forest-green-and-tan quilt. There was a shared night table and lamp in between the beds. The floors were covered with a green-brown-and-tan-patterned carpet.

"Now how many rooms will you folks be needin'?" asked the thin, pasty-complexioned fifty-ish woman behind the desk. The cigarette that dangled between her lips bounced up and down as she spoke.

Abigail "Bunny" Lockheart's eyes greedily surveyed the faces of the seven potential guests. Her graying red hair was up in rollers, and she was wearing a thick pink robe and worn-down slippers. Her face was still slightly wet, and a there were few streaks of cold cream along her jawline that had been missed when she'd quickly wiped her face after hearing the front bell ringing.

Taking a quick look at the full pegboard behind the woman and recalling that the parking lot was empty except for an old Buick, Adam was certain there would be room at the inn.

He turned to Tamiya. "What do you think, three or four?"

"Three," she replied with a teasing wink. "I've forgiven you."

"I'm getting my own room!" Nedry demanded. "I'll pay for it myself."

"Back up to four then."

The manager took an accounting. "A hundred a night room rate."

"Okay."

"Plus," she quickly added, "a twenty-fi—I mean 50 percent surcharge for each extra adult per room."

Since there was nothing printed or in view, Adam decided that the woman set her rates and policies on what she thought the market would bear.

"Twenty-five," he negotiated.

Bunny tightened her face, regarding him with the skepticism of an experienced poker player. "Fine."

"So that's one-twenty-five, one-twenty-five, one-twenty-five, and one hundred for Newt. Four-seventy-five altogether."

As he handed over his MasterCard for processing, he saw the corners of Bunny's eyes crinkle as she extended her bony hand to accept it.

"How long are you folks gonna be staying with us?" she asked.

"Just for the night," Adam confirmed. "We'll be checking out first thing in the morning."

"Are you all some kind of tour group or something?"

"We're heading back to Berkeley. These are my students."

"I see." There was a hint of suspicion and disapproval in her eyes. "Well, there's fresh linens on the bed, towels in the bathroom, and satellite TV except in room one-o-six. That one's broke. And if you need anything, you can just pick up the phone and dial 9, which rings me."

"Do you have room service?" Nedry asked. "I'm starving."

The woman pointed out the window. "Diner's right across the street," she snorted.

Adam looked out the window to the small, white-washed cinderblock building with the neon sign that read "Charlie's Diner." A line underneath the main sign added the slogan: "Best Grub in Town."

"My daughter's a waitress over there. Just tell 'em Bunny sent you."

* * *

Charlie's Diner was a well-worn, but brightly lit eating establishment and gathering place for locals, truckers, and the occasional travelers passing through. Several tables were dispersed around the dining room, and cozy booths lined along two of the walls. Toward the back there was a bar counter with stools and a cash register. Behind the counter was the kitchen with a large black grill top being tended to by a portly short order cook wearing a white T-shirt, a stained apron, and a white paper hat.

As Adam and the students entered the eatery, they were greeted by the sound of country music blaring from the retro jukebox. Most of the tables in the diner were empty. An elderly couple sat in the first booth just to the left of the entrance. A Native American woman and two small children were at a small table a few feet away.

Sitting in the worn booth to the right of the front door were a couple of local redneck types. Carl Junior was a muscular man with a thick handlebar moustache and tattoos up and down his arms. He wore his sandy blond hair in a short mullet. Larry Pickett had a shaved apple-shaped head, a ruddy face, two missing teeth, three days of scraggly beard growth, and a beer belly. Having cleaned their plates of the pork chops, mashed potatoes, and green peas dinner, the two men had already assembled a collection of ten empty Budweiser bottles and were working on two more.

Seeing the newcomers, Carl Junior's eyes immediately went to Tegan's attention-grabbing T-shirt.

Emitting a low whistle he said, "Hey, there, sweetheart, why don't you slide your pretty little be-hind in here?"

"Yeah, I'll give you a place to sit," Larry chuckled with a wink. He slid over to make room.

Tegan looked at the seedy pair. "Eww," she said, turning up her lip.

"Y'all boys leave them tourists alone," said an authoritative voice.

The voice belonged to Sheriff Brock McCain, who was seated at the large round table in the center of the diner. The stoutly built, fifty-four-year-old sheriff wore a neatly pressed khaki-colored uniformed with a six-point star badge on the left chest and patches on the shoulders. His matching Stetson hat and folded Ray-Bans were placed on the table. The sheriff had a rugged, strong-featured face with a hard jawline, wide forehead, steel-colored eyes, and thin, bloodless lips. He wore his gray-peppered brown hair in a regulation crew cut.

"Sure thing, sheriff," said Carl Junior. "We didn't mean no disrespect."

The center table was a beehive of activity with several of the locals seated around. In addition to the sheriff, there was Otis Newhouse, a beefy long-haul truck driver wearing a CAT baseball cap, plaid shirt, and suspenders; "Slim" Petty, a whip thin propane truck driver; Rufus Mullins, a prune-faced farmer in his sixties wearing bib overalls; Bert Dorgan, who ran the barbershop; and Earl Smith, one of the local merchants.

The sheriff's two uniformed deputies were also at the table. Wally Deavers was a gangly twenty-eight-year-old with oily dark hair and a pencil-thin moustache. Twenty-year-old Brock McCain, Jr., "Little Brock" or "LB" for short, looked like a younger, lumbering version of his father.

Taking the scene in, Tegan rolled her eyes and remarked, "God, it's *Mayberry Meets the Twilight Zone.*"

"Well, I bet they got all kinds of good down-home cookin' in here," Shaggy said, patting his thin stomach.

"Just find a seat anywhere," a squeaky-pitched voice called out to the new arrivals.

The attractive, slightly plumpish young woman who waved to them was in her early twenties. Her pale complexion was almost vampiric and bright-red lipstick set off her heart-shaped lips. She wore a pink uniform with apron and had her carrot-colored hair pulled up in a bun under her waitress cap. The name "Ginger" was embroidered on the uniform in burgundy thread. There was little doubt that she was Bunny's daughter.

As Adam and the students made their way to one of the open booths, they could overhear snippets of conversation from the main table.

"It was bad enough where it was some chickens," Rufus, the farmer, was saying. "But last week one of my cows went missing. I'm tellin' ya, sheriff, we got somebody poaching livestock."

"And I told you last week, Rufus, it was more'n likely some wayward coyotes," Sheriff McCain said. "You probably got holes in your fence that need fixin'."

"Ain't no stinkin' coyotes attacking my cattle. Somebody's poachin' 'em. And I ain't the only one. I been hearing about missing livestock as far away as Sedona."

"Sheriff's right," another voice chimed in. "After the drought we've been havin' this summer, I wouldn't be surprised if there's coyotes out there packin' up. If they get hungry enough, a pack of 'em'll take down a full-grown cow for sure."

"Don't go getting' rumors started, Slim. I don't need folks goin' off half cocked and start shooting up coyotes."

The sheriff eyed the owner of the local gun shop. "And, Earl, I know right now you're thinking' a rumor like this would be good for your ammo business."

LB kept cutting his eyes over to the booth where the pretty college girls were sitting.

The bubbly waitress came up to the booth. "How's everyone doin'?"

"You must be Mrs. Lockheart's daughter," Adam said.

"Folks, just call her Bunny. But that's right, I'm Ginger."

"She said to tell you she sent us. We're all staying at the inn."

"Well then, welcome to Redbone. Now what can I get you nice folks to eat?"

A half hour later the travelers were enjoying meals of hamburgers, chicken, meat loaf, biscuits, fries, baked beans, potatoes with gravy, grilled vegetables, and coleslaw.

"Now this is what I call stick-to-your-ribs chow," Shaggy proclaimed, finishing up his third hamburger. "Dude, I am stuffed."

"Who would have thought somebody as skinny as you could put away so much food?" Tamiya said, shaking her head.

"Hey, after all these weeks on the road and whatever some of that stuff we were eatin' down in Central America, I can take on just about anything."

"How 'bout a Scooby snack?" CJ remarked.

"Bring 'em on, dude!"

"Haven't these people ever heard of salads?" Tegan said as she picked over her grilled chicken. "They eat like pigs."

"Tastes good to me," Nedry said. He had consumed two large squares of savory meat loaf bathed in ketchup.

"Of course, it does."

"I don't think one diner meal is going to ruin your perfect figure," said Yeardley.

"You never know."

Ginger came up to the table. "I hope you folks are leaving room for dessert," she said. "We got some fresh homemade lemon meringue pie."

"Awright!" exclaimed Shaggy.

"Where in the world are you gonna put it?" Tamiya asked.

"Oh, I got room."

As Ginger left to cut up the pie, Sheriff McCain came up to the booth.

"You folks new in town?" the law officer asked in a voice that was gruff with a twang of hospitality.

"My students and I are just passing through," Adam replied.

"Headin' to where?" There was just a slight bit of an interrogatory tone in his voice.

"Back to Berkeley."

"Berkeley?"

"Yes, the university." Adam extended his hand. "Dr. Adam Landis."

The sheriff shook Adam's hand, then looked around the table at the youngsters. "So you're what, their teacher."

"Professor . . . of anthropology."

"Best prof at the school," Shaggy chimed in.

The sheriff eyed the young man, immediately sizing him up as a stoner type. "And what brings you and your students to our little town here professor?"

"We're headed back from an archeological dig in the Yucatán Peninsula. We needed to stop for the night, and this town looked pretty inviting."

"That it is?" the sheriff said with a little pride. "Well, if you need anything, we're in the station house across the way. Otherwise y'all have a pleasant stay." He tipped his hat. "Ladies."

As the sheriff left to rejoin the locals at their favorite table, Tegan rolled her eyes and put her index finger into her open mouth in a "gag me" gesture.

6

The residual elation of the five-thousand-dollar payday was still swirling around in Loco Joe's head. He was already making plans for what he'd be buying—some new overalls, shirts, boots and caps, lumber and supplies to patch up the house, a flat screen TV and a satellite dish.

He stood outside the corral, gently stroking Lucile's tangled coat with a metal bristled horse brush.

"Soon as that there college professor 'thenticates our discovery, we's gonna be famous, Lucy," Joe chuckled to the burro. "And there's gonna be even more money. Maybe a million dollars."

Lucile brayed softly in response.

"I'm gonna get us a bigger place, and you're gonna have all the space you could ever want."

He looked up at the sky.

"Yep, after all these years of knockin' around, we both deserve a nice place to live out our twilight years."

The burro's ears suddenly perked straight up to attention. She took an uneasy step back.

"What is it, girl?" Loco Joe asked.

Pacing nervously, Lucile backed up a few more steps.

Loco Joe grabbed the mule's bridle. "Whoa, steady, girl. Steady yourself."

The two dogs, Cain and Thanos, who had been lying on the ground asleep were suddenly up on their feet and growling.

"Now what all's got into you two?"

The pit bulls' growls turned into barks, and Loco Joe could see that their attention was focused out into the darkness. Both massive dogs, each of which weighed nearly ninety pounds, were chained to an iron stake that had been hammered into the ground. They had pulled the fifteen-foot length of heavy gauge chains taut and were straining to break loose.

The old man held up a kerosene lantern and peered out into the night. "Who's out there?" he demanded loudly.

Only his echo came back.

Loco Joe reached down and unhooked the heavy chains from the stake. Barely able to control the savagely barking dogs, he said, "I'm warnin' you one last time. You'd best show yerselves or I'm gonna put my babies on you!"

He thought he could just make out a shadow moving in the dark.

"There you is!" Loco Joe exclaimed. He let go of the chains. "Cain! Thanos! Go get 'im!"

Freed from their master's hold, the massive pit bulls tore off in a fury, dragging the heavy chains behind them. Within two seconds, they both disappeared into the darkness.

Loco Joe heard the sounds of attack as the dogs set upon their quarry. Then a second later, there was a snapping sound accompanied by a bloodcurdling dog yelp. It was quickly followed by another yelp and a ripping sound.

Silence.

"C-Cain? Thanos!? Can you hear me?" the old man inquired nervously. "You-you two okay out there?"

Loco Joe's eyes widened as two hulking figures emerged from the darkness. His mouth was working to form words, but nothing would come out.

Lucile whinnied loudly and reared back on her hindquarters. There was a whooshing sound followed by a heavy thud, and the burro's cries were cut short midwhinny.

Loco Joe saw his longtime friend and companion crumple and fall over into the dirt.

"L-Lucile?" The old man was backing away. "Lucile."

Then a dark blob in the shadow turned toward him. There was a momentary glint of a red reflection.

"What-what is you?" the old man asked, eyes widening in terror.

The silence of the night was shattered by a long, tortured scream.

7

At just after daybreak, the morning light poured into room 105 of the Redbone Inn. As Adam slowly awoke, he could feel Tamiya's firm naked breasts crushed up against his bare chest. It felt good.

It had been the first time in weeks that the couple had shared a real bed. Before that it had been sleeping in sleeping bags, cots, hammocks, or in the RV. None of which had been terribly conducive to lovemaking—especially with the students in close proximity. They'd snuck in a few awkward, quickie sessions here and there and had stolen away one evening for an adventurous outdoor encounter. But that had been it.

At that moment they were covered only by the thin motel sheet. Tamiya was curled up against him, a blissful smile on her lips.

"Morning, handsome," she purred, her eyes still closed.

"Morning," he replied. "How long have you been awake?"

"A few minutes. But I was just nice and comfy here."

"So you're not mad at me anymore?"

"You couldn't tell last night."

"I wasn't sure."

Tamiya rolled over on top and straddled him with her long, bronze legs. She pinned his hands down with hers. "We could do it again before the kids wake up."

"You are an aggressive little primate this morning, aren't you?"

"Did you just call me a little mon—"

She was cut short by a loud, insistent knock at the door.

"Great. They're awake," Tamiya said. She slid off Adam and rolled over onto the bed.

"What are they doing up so early?" Adam complained.

He slipped on a pair of boxers and started toward the door.

Tamiya slid down and hid under the sheets. "Just tell them we'll leave in an hour and then come back to bed."

Another hard knock came at the door.

Pulling a t-shirt over his head, Adam acknowledged, "Okay, okay."

He opened the door, expecting to admonish one of his students. Instead he found himself looking directly into a pair of dark aviator-style sunglasses. His eyes trailed up to the six-pointed star badge that was pinned to a khaki-colored Stetson.

"Sheriff McCain?" the university professor was surprised and a little confused.

"Professor, I'm gonna need you and your students to come down to the station with me."

"Is there a problem?"

"I'll be the one asking the questions." The sheriff looked past the professor and saw the outline of Tamiya's naked form under the bedsheet. "You too, ma'am."

* * *

Fifteen minutes later Adam, Tamiya, and the students were all sitting in the sheriff's station.

Constructed of cinderblock with a flat roof, the modest, single-level station hadn't changed much in appearance in the past fifty years. There were two deputy's desks, a booking area, and two holding cells in the main area. The sheriff had a small private office off to the side. In the back was a storage room, a padlocked weapons closet, and a tiny restroom. The landline phone system was more than thirty years old, and the two bulky computers were practically antiques. Remodeling had consisted of a fresh coat of light blue-gray paint every four or five years.

"Okay, sheriff," Adam said, "now that you've gotten us up and brought us down here, can you please tell me what this is all about?"

"There's been a homicide," the thick-necked sheriff said pointedly.

Twenty-nine years before Brock McCain had started his career as a cadet with the Phoenix Police Department. After fifteen years on the force, he'd worked his way up to sergeant before switching over to the Arizona State Trooper Division. He'd put in twenty-five years of combined service before taking an early retirement, which allowed him to continue drawing 65 percent of his former salary.

The quiet life of being the local sheriff suited him. The cost of living was low, and in Redbone he was a big fish in a very small pond. He could regale the locals with tales from his days on the force and hunt and fish at his leisure, all while drawing a supplemental sheriff's salary. Beyond vandalism, petty theft, domestic disputes, and minor nuisances, crime in the bucolic desert town was practically nonexistent.

But now he had a fresh homicide in his backyard, and that wasn't sitting right with him.

"A what?" Tamiya asked in surprise.
"A homicide, young lady," the sheriff said. "A murder."
"I know what it means."
"What does that have to do with us?" asked Adam.
"The murder victim was one Joe Cunningham. Commonly referred to as Loco Joe."

"That old prospector?"

"So you do know him."

"We met him. Once."

"And I've got a witness that puts you folks out at his place yesterday evening."

"Right, so?"

"I guess that detail must have slipped your mind when I asked last night what you folks were doing in town."

"Not really. Like I said we were on our way to school, and we stopped off to visit Mr. Cunningham. He'd been calling my office for more than a week and leaving messages."

"And why was that?"

"He thought he'd made a significant anthropological find and wanted to show it to me. I'm an expert in that field."

"And had he? Made some great find that is?"

"No," Adam lied. "His 'discovery' was just an assortment of unrelated parts and malformed bones. Nothing really."

Out of the corner of his eye, Adam saw Tamiya's head whip around to look at him. He felt her stare burning into the side of his face.

"Yeah, that'd be Loco Joe. Been chasin' every wild-ass idea since I've known him," the sheriff said with a nod. "So then what happened? How'd he take it when you told him his discovery was worthless? Was he angry? Did the two of you argue?"

"No, of course, not. We chatted for a while. He thanked us for going out of our way to come see him. Then we left."

"And what time was that?"

"Just before sunset, maybe eight o'clock, eight fifteen."

"And he was alive then?"

"Of course, he was alive."

"Joe's place is less than fifteen minutes from here. According to Bunny over at the inn, you folks didn't roll in until after 10:00."

"Because we got lost and ended up driving around in circles for more than an hour. The gas station attendant can confirm this. He and some of his friends found us and brought us into town."

"Billy Lightfoot? Them Renegade biker boys ain't nothing but delinquents, always up to no good. What were they doin' out there at that time of night?"

"I couldn't tell you."

The sheriff looked away from Adam. His deep-set cold gray eyes trailed over to Tamiya. She returned his stare in kind, challenging him. The sheriff looked hard into the eyes of each of the students, taking a full ten seconds on each face. He was testing to see if one of them would break ranks.

"And all of you agree on these facts?" he asked. "Every last detail?

"Just like the teach says," Shaggy spoke up. "Old dude was alive and kickin' when we left."

The sheriff gave Shaggy a disapproving scowl. "What about the rest of you?"

Nedry looked like he was about to throw up, but CJ caught his eye and shot him a threatening look.

They all backed up Adam's account.

"You know . . . I could interrogate each of you individually," the sheriff said. "If even one detail of your stories didn't match up to my satisfaction, I could detain the lot of you."

The sheriff looked at Nedry. "What about you, son? Do you concur with what the professor here is telling me? Last chance."

"Y-yeah, I concur with it," Nedry said. "Everything."

The sheriff sat back and adjusted his Stetson. "Fine."

"Good," Adam said. He started to rise. "Then if we're done here, my students and I need to get back on the r—"

The sheriff cut him off. "I said all right on your story. I didn't say you were free to leave town."

"Why?"

"I got a fresh homicide case here, son. To the best of my knowledge, you and your students were the last people to see the victim alive."

"But we didn't have anything to do with it."

"Maybe."

"Do you think we'd have come into town if we had committed a murder?"

"People have done stranger."

"You can't just keep us here," Tamiya complained, getting up out of the chair.

"Actually, by law I can hold all of you as suspects for up to forty-eight hours without a charge."

"Forty-eight hours?" Nedry whined.

"This is insane," said Tamiya. "We have to get back to school."

"Don't get your knickers in a knot, ma'am," Sheriff McCain said. "I said by law I *could* hold you for forty-eight hours. I didn't say I would. But I do have to conduct my preliminary investigation. Then if your story checks out, you'll be free to leave with the provision that you can be subpoenaed back if we need you."

"How long will that take?"

"Difficult to tell. I haven't gotten to the crime scene yet, just sent my deputy out. But my guess is we'll be done with our initial work by end of day. So I'd say you should plan to spend one more night in our fair town."

"Another night?"

Everyone started to protest.

"Now settle down, folks. You might think I'm just a hick sheriff in a little backwater town, but I am the law here. I've gotta whole load of work to do on this case—evidence to gather, pictures to take, interviews to conduct. Small, peaceful town like this, something like this don't ever happen. So you should be happy I ain't keeping y'all here longer. And it's not like I'm locking you up. I just need you to be available for the next twenty-four hours. And don't worry, I'll talk to Bunny and get you reduced rates for your rooms.

The sheriff's radio crackled.

He unclipped the police radio from his belt, held it up to his mouth, and pressed the talk button. "McCain." There was a response that sounded unintelligible, but the sheriff knew who it was. "LB, did you get out there?"

LB's cracking voice could be heard over the radio. "Y-yes, sir."

"Well, what is it, boy?"

"Sheriff . . . Dad, I think you better come out and see this for yourself."

Once they were allowed to leave, Adam and the students headed back over to the inn.

As soon as they were a reasonable distance from the station, Tamiya turned around to confront Adam.

"What the hell are you thinking!" she demanded.

"What?"

"Why didn't you tell him about that thing in the cooler?"

"Because," Adam explained, "he would have taken it as 'evidence' and done god knows what with it."

"So you lied to him! And not only that you set me and the students up as accessories?"

"You're not accessories."

"We lied to a police officer. I'm pretty sure that's perjury."

"Perjury is only if you're under oath."

"Adam, cut the legalese crap. We're breaking the law and you know it."

"Look, Tam, I don't know what that creature is, but we can't just turn it over to some small-town sheriff."

"That *creature* is a hoax, Adam. And for all you know, it might be the motive for the murder. Maybe one of Loco Joe's drinking buddies, Crazy Tom or Dummy Dan, killed him for it."

"I don't think the specimen had anything to do with him getting murdered."

"You don't know that."

"Fine, I don't know! But why don't we just see what the sheriff comes back with first. If he asks for the specimen or it seems like it does have something to do with the case, then we can turn it over. But I'd rather not just volunteer it. The most important thing is to get it into a lab."

"Dude, we're at the center of a friggin' murder investigation," said Shaggy. "But don't worry, we'll back you up, prof."

"Nobody committed a murder, Shags," said CJ. "Our timing just sucks."

"I can't believe that old man is dead," Yeardley said. "We just saw him yesterday."

"I told you we shouldn't have stopped, Adam," said Tamiya. "Now look at this mess."

"How was I supposed to know this would happen? Anyway, it's only one more day. After that we'll be cleared, and we can get back on the road, *with* the specimen."

"Is that all the hell you can think about?"

"Tam, it could be something major. You know that."

"I can assist you with the lab work, professor," Yeardley volunteered.

"Thanks, I'd appreciate the help."

"God, what an apple polisher," Tegan said under her breath.

"D'you think they're serving breakfast at the diner yet?" Nedry asked.

"Sausage, eggs, and pancakes are probably cookin' on the griddle right now, dude," said Shaggy.

8

As Sheriff McCain's cruiser pulled up to Loco Joe's shack, he could see LB waving his hands above his head as he came out to meet him.

A former offensive lineman on the Carson Flats High School football team, the burly six-foot-three inch, 260 pounder had softened up from his playing days. His lumbering frame, beefy face, and close-cropped dirty-blond hair made him look every bit the stereotypical dumb jock.

LB hadn't been good enough to make it into a college program. So after he'd earned his two-year associate's degree in criminal justice from Central Arizona Community College, his dad pulled the necessary strings and got him the deputy job.

The deputy had only been on the job for about six months. Up until then the highlights of his career had been issuing tickets, chasing down a group of thirteen-year-old vandals who had been spray-painting around town, recovering several lost pets, intervening in endless domestic disputes, and breaking up a drunken bar fight between two men in their seventies.

Nothing had prepared him for the scene he'd been combing through for the past twenty-five minutes.

"You look pretty peaked there, son," the sheriff said, "like you gonna start pukin' at any minute."

"I already did," LB reluctantly admitted, "twice."

"Well, let's see whatcha got."

"It's around back. I called the coroner from over in Carson Flats. He's on his way, but he won't be here for another couple of hours."

As they came around the back of the shack in the direction of the corral, the sheriff could hear the buzzing of flies as the stench of blood, urine, and donkey manure wafted up into his nostrils. However, the smells were just a prelude.

The crime scene was like something out of a slaughter house. The two dead pit bulls, still with their chains around their necks, looked as if they'd been put in a blender. One of the dog's midsection was completely caved in. Broken, blood-coated rib bones could be seen poking through the dark tan hide. The other canine had been literally torn in half lengthwise, as if someone had grabbed it by the top and bottom teeth and pulled it apart. Gelatinous internal organs could be seen where the halves of the animal lay open and exposed. Just inside the corral, the old mule lay on the ground. She had been decapitated. A trail of thick, coagulated blood led from the body to the head, which was lying a few feet away. A tangle of torn tissue and veins protruded from the bottom of the head.

Finally there was Loco Joe. The old man was propped up against the corral post, his face slack and frozen in a death stare. A thick, foamy pinkish fluid had oozed from his half-open mouth and dried on his chin. His skull had literally been crushed like a soft-boiled egg and chunks of brain matter had mingled with the blood running down his shoulder. Just below his breastbone, his insides had been hollowed out, like it had been scooped out with a shovel. Had the spinal column not been mostly intact, the body would have been in two pieces.

"Lord in heaven," remarked Sheriff McCain.

"Somethin' tore 'em all up, Dad."

"I can see that." The sheriff surveyed the horrific scene. "What the hell could have done this?"

"Maybe a grizzly?"

"In these parts? I ain't never seen no animal do this kind of damage. Looks more like the handiwork of some crazed killer."

"I checked the house, it didn't look like a robbery."

"Not surprising. Loco Joe barely had two nickels to rub together?"

The sheriff then looked over in the direction of the dilapidated storage shed. "What about the shed? Did you check that out?"

"Uh, no, sir."

The sheriff and deputy went over to the shed and opened the door. The strong odor of formaldehyde met them head on. Shining their flashlights into the darkened room, they could see that the place had been ransacked. Tools were thrown about. Worktables were turned over. Stuffed animals had been pulled down and torn open; a large cylindrical jar lay shattered on the ground.

"Somebody was after somethin'," the sheriff remarked.

* * *

That evening Adam and the students were back at the diner. They had spent most of the uneventful day waiting for the sheriff to return; however they hadn't heard anything since that morning. There were a few people in the eatery, but it was otherwise quiet. A somber mood seemed to have settled over the town. News of Loco Joe's murder had quickly spread, and people were spooked.

"Great, just great," CJ complained. "Stuck for another day in a greasy spoon in Jerkwater USA. I was hoping to salvage what was left of my summer."

"You got plans, bro?" Shaggy asked.

"Headin' down to Malibu to chill at the beach and catch some late-summer waves with my buds."

"Headin' to 'the Bu'! I bet you got some fine chickas lined up to party with ya." Shaggy held up a hand to high-five the water polo jock.

CJ just left him hanging.

"I got three weeks before school starts back up, and I'm gonna make the most of it."

"Well, you've officially brought your grade up to a gentleman's C, Mr. Jankovich," Adam said. "So I'm sure your coach will be happy."

"Yeah, thanks."

"I hope you also learned something."

"I did. I learned that Intro to Anthro ain't an easy A."

Shaggy laughed. He held up his hand again. "C'mon, dude, gimme some lovin'."

CJ gave him a pitty-slap.

"What about you, princess?" Shaggy asked Tegan. "What are you gonna do with your sexy self the rest of the summer?"

"Go someplace clean and civilized," she said drolly.

"Oh, but you're gonna miss us when we're gone."

"Hardly."

The front door to the diner opened, and the sheriff and deputy entered. Both men looked exhausted.

The sheriff pointed the deputy in the direction of the center table where several of the locals from the previous night were seated and drinking beers. The men had been quietly but anxiously awaiting news about the murder.

The sheriff headed over to the booth where Adam and the students were seated. He pulled up a chair and sat down.

"Well, I'm satisfied you folks didn't have anything to do with what happened up there," he said.

"What did happen?" Adam asked.

"Investigation is still ongoing. But you all will be free to leave in the morning."

"Why can't we leave tonight?" Tamiya asked.

"Miss, I been out at a grisly murder scene all day, and I am tired. I gonna need y'all to check in with me before you get on the road in the morning. One, so I can get your official statements and all your contact information."

"And two?"

"And two, because I want to make doubly sure I ain't lettin' a guilty party slip out of here. As bleary-eyed as I am, I need the night to make sure I'm clearheaded when I release you folks."

"So about Mr. Cunningham?" Adam returned to the original question.

"Believe me you don't wanna know the gory details, professor."

"But you don't think we . . ."

"If I did, you wouldn't be goin' anywhere now, would you? Truth is if I didn't know better, I'd think he was attacked by a grizzly. Except we don't get bears in these parts and I didn't see any paw prints. Only other explanation is maybe we got some crazed killer or killers out there 'cuz somebody got in and ransacked his shed. My guess is they were probably looking through his junk for somethin' to sell for drug money."

"Is there anything that we can do?"

"You just make yourselves available to me if and when I need you."

"Of course."

The sheriff got up and tipped his hat to the females. Then he went over to join his neighbors and deputies for conversation and a late meal.

9

Following dinner, Adam and the students headed back to the inn. They did a quick check on the RV; then Adam told everyone to turn in early. He wanted to meet with the sheriff first thing in the morning and then get on the road. The sooner the town of Redbone was in their rearview mirror, the better.

Yeardley and Tegan were changing into their pajamas for the evening.

"Three weeks of third world living and this isn't much better," Tegan complained.

"You didn't like the Yucatán?" asked Yeardley.

"Duh, right. Crawling around in the dirt looking for bits of bone, with a bunch of sweaty little men with gold teeth leering at my ass, is not exactly my idea of a good time."

"Then why'd you volunteer to come?"

"Why do you think?"

"And you thought that going on a Central American dig was going to get you close to Dr. Landis?"

"Like you didn't?"

"I'm gaining experience so I can apply to be his *research* assistant. I wasn't the one prancing around in Daisy Dukes."

"Sweetheart, the shy geek girl thing ain't working. I've seen you 'researching' the professor's perfectly chiseled face and tight butt."

Yeardley had no intention of admitting to her schoolgirl crush on Dr. Landis. "He's into Tamiya."

"Yeah, I kinda finally figured that one out. Wasted half my summer doin' so."

As she was pulling on her top, Tegan thought she noticed a shadow moving outside the window. "Hey, somebody's out there."

"Out where?" Yeardley asked.

"Creeping around outside the window."

Both women went to the window and peered out into the dark. The alley that ran behind the inn was meagerly illuminated by a single low-wattage lantern.

At first they saw nothing. Then in the shadows about fifty feet away, they noticed a long-haired man sitting on a motorcycle and smoking a cigarette.

"It's that Indian guy from the gas station," Tegan whispered giddily.

Yeardley, who had stripped down to a bra and panties, quickly covered her thin frame. "What's he doing back there?"

"Probably trying to get a peek."

"We should call the sheriff."

"Why?"

"Because he might be a stalker or a pervert or something."

Tegan grabbed her jeans and quickly started putting them on.

"What are you doing?" Yeardley asked, alarmed.

"He's kinda cute."

Tegan unlatched the window and began sliding it up.

"Are you crazy? We're supposed to stay in the room."

"Who are you, my mother?"

She slipped out of the window and into the alley.

Tegan came up behind Billy, who was straddling his bike and had his back to her. "So did you get a good eyeful?" she asked, teasingly.

Billy turned around, startled. "Huh?" Then his eyes recognized her. "Oh, hey."

"Don't try to tell me you weren't."

"Weren't what?"

"Creeping around outside our window, pervert."

He smiled. "*You* snuck up on me. I was just sittin' here takin' a smoke."

"And you didn't notice the two nubile young women undressing in that window not fifty feet away?"

He held up a hand. "Honest Injun."

"Riiiiight."

"Hey, if you want to go back and put on another show, I'll pull up a seat."

"Show's over, bad boy."

She walked around to the front of the bike and leaned onto the handlebars, her well-shaped breasts facing him. "So is this what you folks in *Redbone* do for excitement on a Saturday night?"

"Pretty much."

"Boring."

"You don't think much of this town, do you?"

Tegan shrugged, "Can't wait to fly this burg. Which we will be doing tomorrow."

"Wish I could. But not much chance of that."

"Just a small-town boy?"

"And you're a city girl."

"Journey." Tegan nodded in approval. They were both familiar with the rock group's hit song *Don't Stop Believin'* even though they had inverted the boy-girl roles.

"It's a classic. Even out here."

Tegan looked into his eyes. "You know, for an Indian . . . or I guess the PC to say is Native American. Anyway for a Native American, you have the bluest eyes."

"That's 'cuz I'm a half-breed."

"Half-breed?"

"Yep, my ole man was a white dude. Not that I remember all that much about him. Y'know that old cliché, he went out for a six pack and smokes one afternoon and never came back."

"Sucks."

"I was four at the time. My ma always said I had his eyes. Course it could have been worse. I could've got his blond hair like my little sister."

"So what's the deal with you and your buddies riding around on these bikes with your little custom paintjobs? Are you trying to look like a badass biker gang or somethin'?"

Billy patted his gas tank. "These ain't Harley's fräulein, they're dirt bikes. A couple of us are trying to qualify for the Motocross X Games."

"You mean like on ESPN?"

"Yep."

"You any good?"

"Real good. Maybe I can give you a ride sometime."

She smiled flirtatiously. "You are a bad boy."

Billy's cheeks reddened. "I was talkin' about lettin' you ride on the back."

Just then they were interrupted by the loud sound of banging against metal.

"Is that another one of your friends back here?" Tegan asked accusingly.

Billy shook his head. "No, just me."

There was another loud banging of metal, followed by the sound of glass shattering. They were both concerned.

Billy looked in the direction of the noise. "It's coming from over in the back parking lot."

"Our camper's parked around there."

"I'll check it out."

Billy got off his bike and headed toward the lot, which was around the corner about twenty-five yards away. Tegan followed a few steps behind.

A single, low-powered streetlamp meagerly illuminated the small lot. The cracked asphalt had faded white lines denoting seven spaces. A broken down 1987 green Chevy Impala and the Winnebago were the only vehicles currently occupying spaces.

The RV's window had been smashed in and the rear door was open. In the dim light, Tegan and Billy could see the outline of a figure at the back of Winnebago. They could also hear the sounds of someone rummaging around.

"Somebody's tryin' to steal your ride," Billy whispered to Tegan.

"Who is it?" she whispered back.

"I don't know." Then he yelled at the would-be carjacker. "Hey, man, what're you doing!"

The black mass of a figure turned around.

Billy's eyes widened in disbelief, and he took an unsteady step back.

The crouching creature slowly stood to its full height. Billy had to tilt his head up to see the dark outline atop the shoulders where its face should be. Although the creature was in silhouette, it was evident that it was broad and thickly muscled. Light-reflective red eyes seemed to glow back at Billy.

Unfurling a pair of massive batlike wings, the creature issued a low, warning growl.

"What . . . the . . . sh—"

Billy's voice was already being drowned out by Tegan's piercing scream.

With unexpected speed and savagery, the black mass lunged at the pair. A clawed hand the size of a catcher's mitt clamped around Tegan's throat, cutting her off mid-scream. The creature's other hand swatted Billy aside like an insignificant gnat.

The powerful blow knocked the young half-breed back ten feet and to the ground. Still holding Tegan by the throat, the creature turned away and headed back over to the RV.

Billy's head was swirling in pain from the creature's heavy blow. He looked up to see Tegan struggling to get free of her captor, who was dragging her behind him like a potato sack.

Looking around in desperation, Billy spotted a rusted tire iron lying just a few feet away from him. It was a discarded remnant from an unsuccessful attempt to replace one of the abandoned Impala's flat tires. He grabbed up the heavy rusted tool and gripped it in his right hand. Scrambling to his feet still dazed, Billy charged after the creature.

Billy swung the tire iron into the back of the creature's head with all his might.

There was a hard THUNKK of iron against skull. However, it barely fazed the creature, which whipped its head around to confront the attacker.

The creature released Tegan, letting the terrified girl drop to the ground as it turned its attention fully to Billy.

As adrenaline infused, fight-or-flight instincts started overtaking him; Billy backed up, the tire iron still firmly grasped in his hand. Before he was able to take three steps, a second shadowy figure dropped from the sky, directly behind him. It was another creature of similar size. A second later, a third creature landed. He was surrounded by the three winged creatures.

They began closing in on him. Billy held the tire iron up in a threatening posture, but he may as well have been holding up a toothpick. He could hear the hot, low growls emanating from all three of the imposing creatures, their glowing red eyes filled with murderous intent.

Just then, several outside lights flickered to life. The sound of running footfalls shuffling against the gravel and dirt could be heard up the alley. Alerted by the screams, at least ten townies had poured out from the nearby buildings.

Anxious voices mingled together. *"What's going on out here? I heard a scream? Somebody's fightin'? Call the sheriff."*

Quickly, the first creature barked a command to the others in something that sounded to Billy like a foreign language.

The creature to the right of Billy turned away and bounded over to the RV. It reached into the back of the vehicle, tore the lid off a large cooler, and withdrew something that was wrapped in plastic.

The first creature spotted Tegan who was trying to crawl away. He viciously yanked her back by her long blond hair, nearly tearing it out.

"No!" Tegan shrilled in pain and terror.

The massive, seven-foot-tall creature scooped the petite, five-foot-five-inch teenager up and wrapped her in its thick, powerful arms.

"No please!" Tegan shrieked. "Billy, help me!"

Throwing himself into the creature, Billy grabbed Tegan's arms in the attempt to pull her free. "Let her go, man," he shouted.

Screaming and kicking hysterically, Tegan was desperately fighting to save herself. She clawed her hands into Billy's forearms holding on with a white-knuckled grip.

The creature unfurled its wings to full span, and with one powerful flapping motion, it took to the air, carrying a wailing Tegan with him.

As Tegan was ripped from Billy's grasp her long nails raked across and into his bare forearms, tearing bloody, four-inch long claw marks into his flesh. That stinging pain, however, was instantly forgotten as a cold, clawed hand clamped around Billy's neck like a steel vice. With one hand, the last of the creatures held him two feet off the ground, his feet dangling helplessly.

Billy could see its red eyes in the dark and feel its warm, humid breath on his face. The creature's lips curled back revealing a set of saliva-coated fanged teeth.

"What's all this ruckus back here?" a voice shouted from about thirty yards away. The first of the townies had come around the buildings and were approaching the commotion.

Out of time, Billy's attacker flung him aside. There was a cracking sound as one of Billy's ribs was fractured on impact. The back of his head hit the asphalt a split second later. As pain raced through his body like white-hot electricity, the last thing the young man was able to make out as he looked up into the night sky, were the three creatures flying off into the darkness, carrying Tegan with them.

Then blackness overtook him.

10

A chill rose in the air as the trio of creatures glided silently across the clear night sky. The only sound was the occasional flapping of wings.

They had been flying for nearly fifteen minutes, covering miles of distance. One of the creatures was flying out in the lead, and the other two were flanking about twenty yards back. The creature on the left was holding the carcass, still wrapped in the specimen bag. The one on the right was cradling its human captive.

Tegan looked up at the face of her captor. Seeing its red eyes and scale-covered skin, she shrank in terror. Goosebumps rose on her arms from a combination of cold and her fear. She had no idea where they were headed.

As a weak whimper escaped her lips, the petrified young woman could only cringe as she looked down at the ground passing below. Tegan closed her eyes tight and prayed for the nightmare to end.

They were five hundred feet up, and on top of everything else, she had a paralyzing fear of heights.

11

Emerging from the black void of unconsciousness, Billy Lightfoot could hear the sound of voices around him. *"Was some kinda fight . . . wildass Renegades . . . , look at them scratches on his arm . . ."*

The voices merged into faces. Then as the anesthetizing remnants of sleep quickly evaporated, both memories and pain started to return with a vengeance. His head was throbbing, and his ribs felt as if he'd been worked over with a baseball bat.

He tried to sit up.

"Hold on, Billy," said Bunny Lockheart, pressing a cold compress against his head. "Lie back down."

Billy was laid out on the worn couch in the small lobby of the Redbone Inn. A gauze bandage had been placed over a three-inch gash along his right temple. It had been changed once and was already blood-dampened again. His badly bruised ribs had also been wrapped. Since the closest doctor was thirty miles away, the motel manager was tending to him. The fresh cigarette dangling from her lips was dropping ashes on his chest.

"Wha . . . where?" Billy started asking.

"Let me ask the questions, son?" came Sheriff McCain's stern voice as his face appeared over the young man. The sheriff had pulled up a chair beside the couch. "You wanna tell me what all happened out there?"

"Huh?" Billy's brain was still swirling and trying to assemble fragments of memory through a blinding headache.

"Sounded to me like a bunch of 'em fightin' when we got out there, sheriff," said Slim who was standing among the gawking locals. "A bunch of commotion and screamin'."

"Is that what it was, Billy? Were some of you boys back there fightin'?"

"Look to me like he got the bad end of the deal," joked Otis.

The sheriff waved an annoyed hand back at the gawkers. "Would all of you folks just back off and let me conduct this line of questioning?"

"Look at his arms, sheriff," Bunny pointed out.

The sheriff pulled up Billy's right shirtsleeve, revealing the three long scratch marks.

"A woman made them scratches," Bunny concluded. "She was probably trying to fight him off."

"Yeah, we definitely heard a woman screaming his name," Slim added.

"Tegan?" Adam asked as he worked his way to the front of the gathered crowd. He was pulling a visibly upset Yeardley along with him. Tamiya and the other students had also come into the lobby and were standing in with the crowd of onlookers.

"Professor?" Sheriff McCain was surprised to see him there.

"One of my students is missing," Adam said, his eyes frantic with fear and worry.

"She snuck out the window to go talk to him," Yeardley was pointing to Billy. "I knew I shouldn't have let her go."

"And now we can't find her!"

His eyes growing hot with anger, the sheriff turned his attention to Billy. He grabbed the young man by the collar. "All right, Billy," he demanded. "Snap out of it. I want some answers, and I want 'em now. Who was you fightin' and where's that young girl?"

"Wasn't no fight," Billy managed groggily.

"What?"

"Wasn't a fight . . . they attacked us."

"Who attacked you?"

"Those . . . things"

"You ain't makin' much sense, boy. What things?"

"Those . . . creatures . . . monsters."

The gawking onlookers exchanged puzzled looks.

"Monsters?" Otis snorted. "That boy's delirious."

This drew a chuckle from the crowd.

"No," Billy insisted, "that's what it was."

"Monsters?" the sheriff asked.

"Yeah. They was like . . . giant bats."

"Bats? We get bats around here all the time."

"No, they wasn't just bats. They were *like* bats, except they was big as a man . . . bigger."

"What the devil are you talking about, Billy?"

Billy managed to sit up. He propped himself up on his elbow, and his face grew serious. "They had these, these batwings, and they stood upright just like a full-grown man."

"Now let me get this straight, son. You're trying to tell me that you and that girl were attacked by some kind of giant man-bats?"

"Yeah."

Slim, Otis, and several of the others were trying to hold in their laughter.

"Man-bats . . . Is that like the opposite of Batman?" Slim said to Otis.

"Did'ja see Robin too, Billy?" Otis joked.

The sheriff shot a stone-faced glare over to Slim and Otis. "I'm gonna have ta ask you boys to wait somewhere else."

"What'd we do?" Slim asked, pointing innocently to himself.

"Flappin' your gums like a couple of fools while I'm trying to work. Now both of you can go on and get out the door. And that goes for anyone else that can't keep his trap shut."

Slim and Otis begrudgingly left the inn, mumbling along the way.

The sheriff turned his attention back to Billy. "Now is that what you're tellin', Billy? That you was attacked by some kinda giant man-sized monster bats?"

"Sheriff, I know it sounds crazy, but there was three of them things. We saw 'em trying to get into those college folks' camper, and then one of 'em's what carried off the girl. It was like something out of a horror movie. And that's the truth. I'd swear it on a stack of Bibles."

Sheriff McCain looked hard into Billy's eyes for long seconds, not saying a word. Then he finally broke his silence. "Son, what kind of fool do you take me for?"

"I ain't takin' you for a fool, sheriff."

"We got a girl that's missing, and we find you all beaten up with scratches on your arm that look like they were made by a woman with long fingernails."

"She was trying to hold onto me when them things took her and flew off."

"Maybe she was trying to fight you off."

"No, it was them things."

"Shut up with that horseshit, Billy! I ain't got time for this. Now I got two workin' theories here. Theory 1: she found out something that implicated you in Loco Joe's murder so you attacked her, and she was trying to defend herself. Theory 2: Maybe she was with you, and you got into a fight with some of them other hell-raisers, and they got her. Now both of those theories make a hell of a lot more sense than giant monster bats, don't they?"

"I'm tellin' you what I saw!"

"No! What you tellin' me is a pack of crazy ass lies while I'm trying to solve a murder and now a possible kidnapping. Two crimes in two days! I guess you figure if maybe you can get me chasin' my tail, you can slip off to join your buddies, most likely hidin' out somewhere in the desert. Well, it ain't gonna work that way. You've admitted you were the last person to see that girl. So unless or until she shows up, you are our prime suspect in her disappearance. And just to be safe, I'm gonna also call you a 'person of interest' in the murder of Loco Joe."

"I didn't kill that old nut!" Billy protested.

"Well, that's somethin' I'm gonna find out. Now first, I'm gonna have LB here run you over and put you in a cell. Then, I'm gonna round up some volunteers, and we're gonna head out to look for that missin' girl. And you better pray we find her safe, untouched, and alive!

"Sheriff, this is crazy. You're wastin' time with me while them things is out there!"

"Where's your proof, Billy?" the sheriff snapped. "Nobody else saw 'em."

"I saw 'em. They took that girl, and they's probably what kilt Loco Joe. For all we know, they might be comin' back for us. We should be figuring out a way to protect ourselves."

"Oh, we gonna figure out everything, Billy, you can mark my words on that one." The sheriff nodded to his son. "Cuff that boy up."

"C'mon, Billy," LB said as he pulled him up off the couch. The deputy had already taken out his handcuffs and had them dangling from his left hand.

"Don't make this harder on yourself, son," the sheriff warned.

LB started turning Billy around to put on the handcuffs.

"I didn't do nothin'!" Billy insisted as his arms were being pulled around. He threw his head back hard into LB, cracking the deputy's nose, causing him to drop the restraints to the ground.

"Get that boy under control!" the sheriff ordered.

Deputy Wally moved in, pulling out his nightstick.

LB grabbed Billy from behind in a bear hug. "Got somethin' to hide, don't ya, Billy?" he said, blood streaming from his nostrils.

"It wasn't me! It was them bat things!"

The sheriff was out of patience. "I am tired of this bull crap. Wally, shut him up."

Deputy Deavers struck the resisting prisoner hard across the back of the neck with his nightstick. For the second time that night, Billy Lightfoot lost consciousness.

"That's how you do it," Wally smirked to LB.

LB growled as he scooped up his fallen handcuffs. He rolled Billy over onto his stomach and shackled his hands behind his back.

Each deputy reached under an armpit and hoisted Billy up, his knees dragging the ground. The young man's head was slumped forward, and his long hair fell in front of his face.

"Get him outta my sight," the sheriff said with disgust.

The deputies dragged Billy out the front door.

"Sorry you and your students had to see that professor," the sheriff said to Adam.

"Do you really think his friends might have taken Tegan?" Adam asked.

"Billy wouldn't have been fightin' like that if he weren't guilty of somethin'."

"I'm responsible for these kids, sheriff. They're all minors."

"We'll find her."

Tamiya burst forward. "What kind of a sheriff are you?" she demanded. "You just let these hoodlums run around town attacking innocent tourists!"

"Now hold on there, Ms. Dawes," the sheriff put his hands up palms out. "I know all them boys. They're a little wild, but they ain't never done any kind of serious crime before."

"Well, now they've probably kidnapped one of our students, which is pretty damned serious. You should be out there right now looking for her. And if you won't go, we will!"

"Ma'am, the desert and nighttime don't exactly mix. Now we'll go to them boys' houses and question around town. But if somebody's got her out there at night, we ain't gonna find them if they don't wanna be found. We'll head out at first light."

"You'd better find her, and she'd better be okay," Tamiya huffed.

"Sheriff," Adam asked. "What did you make of his story?"

"What, monster man bats?" replied the sheriff. "What would you think?"

12

The nighttime wind ripped through Tegan's tangled blond locks as she lifted her head to tentatively look out into the distance. The cold air stung at her eyes, and she was still trembling.

The desert floor that passed a thousand feet below was etched with deep crevices and fissures. The spiraling rock towers, stone arches, and natural formations dotting the arid landscape had been gradually sculpted over hundreds of millennia.

Tegan's mind swirled with panic as she tried to make sense of what had happened in the last twenty minutes. *Why had these "monsters" taken her? Where were they going? What would they to do to her?*

The thick, scaly hide of her captor scraped against her soft skin. She could hear its steady bull-like breathing between the periodic flapping of wings.

At that moment the creatures slowed and began a sharp descent. She could see that they were approaching a massive stone butte.

Rising up from the desert landscape, the red rock monolith looked like a volcano with the top sliced off. It was 827 feet high from base to summit and its rocky, oval-shaped top was 316 feet in diameter. The shear, clifflike walls dropped almost vertically spreading out just slightly at the base.

Centuries ago the Navajo had named it the "Demon's Tower."

As they got closer Tegan could see what looked to be a cave opening near the base of the butte. Two more of the creatures, wings folded in, were crouched on either side of the cave opening like vigilant sentinels.

The returning creatures maneuvered into a single file formation, flew past the sentinels, and entered the cold, black mouth of the cave.

13

It was after two o'clock in the morning by the time all the excitement had died down and the sheriff had sent everyone home. The students had all gone back to their rooms. Tamiya had offered to stay with Yeardley, who was still shaken up and racked with guilt, but the student had insisted she'd be okay.

When they were finally in the room, Tamiya's dropped the calm demeanor she had been wearing for the last several hours.

"What the hell did you get us into, Adam?" she fumed.

"I'm sorry," he said.

"All of this because you just had to stop."

"I didn't know."

"On top of that, somehow you think that Indian kid might be telling the truth, don't you?"

Adam turned away from her stare.

"Don't you?" she repeated.

"I don't know."

"Then why didn't you say something to the sheriff?"

"About what?" Adam demanded. "That we had a carcass of something in our SUV that may or may not resemble what the kid was talking about. And by the way, we got it from the old man that was murdered yesterday."

"Yes!"

"He said the creatures that attacked were six or seven feet tall, with huge batwings. The specimen we had was less than three feet and didn't have wings. Anyway, you were the one saying the carcass was a hoax."

"It still probably is."

"Look, Tam. If I would have said something to support the kid's story, provided they didn't think I was crazy as well, one of three things would have happened. First, it could have involved us even deeper in the old man's murder, which would keep us here for god knows how long. Second, for all we know the kid is guilty, and we would just be supporting his story. And third, the sheriff probably would want to keep the specimen as evidence in his 'investigation.' Can you imagine how much material would be lost if we left it in their hands."

"You have got to be kidding me," Tamiya said in astonishment. "We've got a student missing, Adam. We have no idea where she is or what could be happening to her. And all you can think about is holding on to your damned specimen!"

"I know she's missing," Adam snapped back. "I'm just as worried about her as you. She's my responsibility. But before we start jumping to conclusions, let's try to be rational. It makes more sense that Tegan told that Billy character about the carcass we got from Joe. Maybe some of his friends did decide to steal it. A fight breaks out, and they took off with the specimen and Tegan. When this Billy regains consciousness, he doesn't want to get in trouble so he makes up the giant bat story loosely based on Tegan's description."

Tamiya looked at him skeptically. "That's what you think happened, really?"

"I don't know. These townies are just a bunch of teenagers bored out of their heads with nothing to do around here. They might have been drinking, who knows. But my guess is the sheriff will have a good idea where to find them."

"I hope you're right. We have a teenager out there somewhere."

"He's gonna take his deputies out at first light, which is like 6:00 AM. If they don't have Tegan back with us by nine, I'll tell him about the specimen, okay?"

"If you don't, I will."

"I'll tell him."

"I just want to get out of this godforsaken place and have this nightmare over and done."

Tamiya sat down on the bed, physically and emotionally drained from the day. She put her head in her hands. "It just keeps getting worse."

Adam sat on the other side of the bed. "It's gonna be okay." He reached over and started to rub her back to comfort her.

She pulled away, shaking her head. "No."

"Tam?"

"Just . . . no."

Still fully clothed, she climbed under the pale-green bedsheets. "I'm just gonna try to sleep for a few hours."

"Okay," he said, starting to get in on the other side.

She turned her back to him. "You can sleep on the floor."

Adam narrowed his eyes. But he wasn't in a mood to fight. Without another word, Tamiya reached over and turned off the lamp.

Adam gathered up a pillow and the green and pink floral comforter and threw them on the floor.

* * *

At just after six the next morning, a frantic knock came at the door. Even though neither Adam or Tamiya had planned to doze for very long, they were both still asleep.

Another knock came.

"Adam?" Tamiya asked, sitting up.

Adam was already getting up from his sleeping spot on the floor.

Tamiya's eyes followed him to the door. "Maybe they found Tegan," she said hopefully.

Adam opened the door to see Shaggy standing in front of him. "Shawn?"

Shaggy was wearing a pair of crumpled yellow shorts and a white wifebeater T-shirt. There was a wild-eyed expression on his face.

"The phones, teach!" the gangly student said excitedly.

"What?"

"The phones. That's how we can find the princess."

Adam still had a confused expression on his face.

"Remember before we left, you used that locator app to program in all of our numbers?" Shaggy continued.

Adam's expression immediately changed. "That's right, it's a GPS tracker."

Tamiya came up to join Adam at the door. "Did they find her?" she asked.

"No," Adam said. "At least we haven't heard anything."

"Then what is it? Why's Shaggy here?"

"Hey, T-Lady," Shaggy said, smiling.

"He has an idea for how we can find Tegan," said Adam. "Wait here a minute."

Adam went over to the nightstand and grabbed up his phone. He was powering it on as he walked back.

"Remember before we left for the Yucatán, I plugged everyone's phone IDs into mine?" he explained to Tamiya. "It was to make sure nobody wandered off and got lost."

By that time the phone app had opened. A 3D relief map appeared on the smartphone's five-inch screen.

They all gathered around the device, which was housed in a rugged titanium case.

A blue dot popped up with a label beside it that read "Adam." Concentric circles began spreading out. Within the closest circle, a purple dot labeled *Tam* popped up followed immediately by a green dot labeled *Shaggy*. Then a cluster of dots red, turquoise, and yellow appeared, labeled *CJ, Newton,* and *Yeardley*.

"Okay, that accounts for everyone here," Adam said.

"We're not seeing Tegan's," said Tamiya. "Maybe her battery is dead, or maybe someone took it. Or maybe she's too far—"

"Give it a minute, Tam. As long as her phone is powered, the app should be able to locate it anywhere in the world. It's widening the search."

The screen refreshed with a new map scaled twenty-five-miles-by-twenty-five-miles. The initial set of dots and names all clustered together as more concentric circles began spreading outward. One mile. Five miles. Ten miles. Then a pink dot labeled *Tegan* popped onto the screen.

"There she is!" Tamiya exclaimed.

Adam noted the coordinates. "According to this, she's about eleven miles northwest of here."

"Let's go tell the sheriff."

"The sheriff and his posse rolled out of here about five fifteen this mornin'," Shaggy said. Then he added, "I was up early."

"You saw them leave?"

"Yep."

"They could be gone for hours," Adam said in frustration. "Shawn, go get changed. Then grab CJ and Newton. We'll leave in ten minutes."

"Leave to go where?" Tamiya asked.

Adam held up his phone. "We know where she is."

"So?"

"So we don't have time to wait around for the sheriff to get back."

"And what if those bikers have her?"

"Or the giant bats?" Shaggy suggested. He gave an exaggerated shudder.

"Shaggy!"

"I know, I know." He laughed. "Just tryin' too keep the mood light."

"Then I'm coming with you," she said to Adam.

"We can take care of this, Tam."

"After the past two days, I'm not trusting you to take care anything."

Tamiya's hazel-eyed stare dared Adam to object.

"Fine. We'll leave Yeardley here. When the sheriff gets back, she can let him know where we went."

14

Over its lifetime, Adam's battered and rusted Winnebago had passed through three previous owners and logged more than 250,000 miles over every imaginable topography. Nevertheless, the desert's rock and sand terrain and the various twists and turns along their route had turned a fifteen-minute drive into a forty-minute expedition.

They came to a stop where the road had run out and the ancient, bone-dry basin spread out before them. Thousands of years before, it had been a massive crystal clear lake teeming with life and surrounded by greenery. Now it was just thousands of acres of sun-bleached sandstone, unusual formations, and a labyrinth of caves and crevasses.

"This looks to be as far as we go," Adam said as he stopped the RV. He shifted the vehicle into park and pulled up the emergency brake.

They all got out of the RV and took a minute to survey the barren, unforgiving terrain. While it was only eight in the morning, the temperature had already climbed to eighty degrees, and the sun was just starting to scorch the sand.

"Welcome to the badlands, people," Shaggy proclaimed, taking in the dry air and scanning the flat, barren landscape that stretched on for miles.

"Where do we even look?" Nedry asked.

"Man, I can see why it'd be easy for them bikers to hide out here," said CJ.

Tamiya looked around. "I don't see any sign of Tegan or anyone for that matter."

Adam looked at the blinking pink GPS dot on his phone screen. "According to this, she should be roughly two hundred and seventy-five yards in that direction." He was pointing down into the valley.

"I don't see anything."

"There are probably hidden paths and crevasses running all over the place."

"What about them biker guys? They could be hidin' out somewhere, waiting to jump us," a sweaty Nedry said nervously.

"We'll just have to be on our guard. C'mon," Adam said. He had already set off down into the valley.

Since there were no obvious paths, it took them nearly fifteen minutes going over hills, around stone formations, and through narrow passages to arrive at the source of the signal. The whole time Adam kept his eyes on the screen, making certain they didn't detour off track. As they got closer, Adam instructed everyone to stay quiet and move slowly as they approached. He strained his ears, expecting to pick up on conversation at any moment.

They saw it.

The Apple iPhone with the rhinestone-encrusted pink case was lying out in the open. There were scuffmarks along the sides of the case, and the screen was shattered. It was a wonder it was still working.

Tamiya picked up the phone. "She must have dropped it."

The phone had fallen out of Tegan's pocket the night before as she was being carried off by the creatures.

"What do we do now?" asked Shaggy.

Adam's green eyes squinted as he scanned the terrain. The stone valley stretched out in all directions. There were probably hundreds of possible hiding spaces. "She might still be close by," he said.

"*If* she's still alive," Shaggy said.

"Dammit, Shaggy!" yelled CJ.

"I'm just sayin' it. Everybody's thinking it."

A look of grave concern came over Adam's face. "We need to spread out and look."

"Where?" asked Tamiya. "It could take hours."

"If we split up we can cover more ground."

"Or get lost too."

"I've got everyone's phone programmed in here. Nobody's gonna get lost. We'll split into three groups. Shawn, you, and Newton take that direction."

"You got it, teach," agreed Shaggy. The seriousness of the situation was growing on him. While they had all been worried about Tegan, a sobering desperation was quickly setting in.

"What about them bikers?"

"Nedry man, I am sick of your moaning and bullshit, which I have had to listen to this whole trip," CJ said. "Tegan is out there missing, dude. Maybe in trouble. So you need to get your fat ass in gear and help us look for her."

Adam pointed to the west. "Tam, you and CJ can head that way." He pointed north. "And I'll go there. Listen, everybody... do not go too far. We'll check in every ten minutes. If anyone sees anything, anything at all, call me. If we can't find anything within an hour, we'll head back."

The three search parties headed off in different directions.

* * *

Initially buoyed by a combination of hope and determination, by the time nearly an hour had passed, emotions had started turning to hopelessness.

They had realized just how vast the desert was. Not just the valley where they were searching, but the miles upon miles of bleak territory surrounding them. Tegan could be anywhere.

Adam was already dreading of what he'd say to her parents. She had been his responsibility, and now she was missing without a trace. For just a second the image of a shallow, rock-covered grave crept into his mind. He quickly pushed it out of his head.

Tamiya had seen Adam's growing concern and desperation, which was why she hadn't tried to talk him out of searching. Of course she was hoping that Tegan was somewhere close to where they found the phone, but as she silently trudged along with CJ over the rocky hills, she began doubting they would simply get lucky.

The Mutt and Jeff duo of Shaggy and Newt were climbing up a hillside to get a better vantage point. During the trip, the gangly redhead had been hoping that Tegan would show some kind of interest in him. He knew that she was after Dr. Landis at first, but it became clear the professor wasn't interested. Then Shaggy figured that Tegan might hook up with CJ because he was the pretty-boy jock. But when that didn't happen, Shaggy started trying to turn on the charm. When she realized it, it didn't take much for her to wrap him around her finger. A flirtatious smile or two and he was off fetching her water like an obedient puppy.

* * *

Once the hour had passed, Adam finally admitted to himself that the search effort was futile. The area was just too vast and the conditions too unforgiving. A few minutes earlier, Yeardley had sent him a text message saying that one of the deputies had just gotten back. Tegan wasn't with him. The sheriff and other deputy had gone off to round up and question a number of Billy's biker friends—all of whom were still at their respective homes in town.

If none of them had her, who did?

He called Tamiya.

"Still nothing," she had said when she answered his call.

"Then we should head back," Adam said in defeat. "Maybe the sheriff can put some kind of search party toge—"

Just then he heard the tinny sound of CJ's frantic voice in the background. "What the hell is that?"

"What's wh—" Tamiya started to ask. Before she could finish her question, it turned into a scream. "Oh my god!"

"Tam!" Adam yelled into the phone. "What is it?"

There was a jumble of voices, and the sound of shuffling. Tamiya cried out, "Get away from it, CJ! Run!"

"Tam! Tam!" Adam yelled again.

"There's more of them!" CJ's voice could be heard saying.

"Oh god, no!" Tamiya's voice gasped.

There was a cry of someone in agony.

"What's going on!" Adam shouted.

Elliot heard something clawing; then Tamiya's voice came back to the phone. "Adam, Adam, they're real . . . they're real . . . Oh god. Please . . ." She sounded desperate.

"Tamiya, what's going on?" Adam was frantic.

Strained tears could be heard in her voice. "Adam, plea—"

The call cut off.

Adam redialed the number. It went straight to voice mail. "No!" he yelled in frustration.

He was already on his feet and running in the direction where Tamiya and CJ had gone to search. He quickly selected another number and dialed.

"Shawn, pick up. Pick up!" Adam implored.

The phone rang once . . . twice . . . three times . . . before going to Shaggy's voice mail. "Yeah, this is Shags . . . but you got my machine—"

He dialed Nedry's number. Two rings then voice mail.

Adam picked up his pace as fear and uncertainty began gripping him. He was in the middle of the desert unable to reach Tamiya or any of the students. The blinding hot sun was beating down on him mercilessly. He was sweating so profusely that his khaki shirt was soaked through. As he ran, he repeatedly called the numbers. No one answered.

Finally he came to the vicinity where Tamiya and CJ had been searching. From that vantage point, he could see in all directions. Cupping his hand over his eyes, he scanned the area.

Then he saw a glint of light reflect off of something metallic about 150 feet to his right.

Racing over he quickly spotted the metallic object—CJ's Berkeley Bears Water Polo logo pin. Looking around, Adam recognized the signs of struggle. There were several footprints and drag marks in the sand between the rocks. There was also a ragged four-inch-long strip of torn fabric that matched the lightweight denim shirt Tamiya had been wearing. But what horrified him most was the blood. Fresh blood was splattered over several of the surrounding rocks, and dripping down the sides. There was a small pool of blood just a few feet away from him. Lying in the blood was a shattered cell phone.

Adam's eyes widened and a sickening nausea overtook him. "No, no, no," he cried.

He called out Tamiya's and CJ's names several times, only to hear the echoes of his own voice come back.

Then he thought of the other two students, Shaggy and Nedry. He still couldn't reach them. He checked the GPS app and saw only Shaggy's green pulsating dot registering. Desperately, he set off to the west.

By the time he arrived at the location twenty minutes later, Shaggy's indicator signal had disappeared. He wasn't able find any trace of the two students.

15

Tamiya could feel herself being dragged along as she slowly began regaining consciousness. She was being taken down a narrow, dimly lit passage. The dark gray shear rock walls on either side of her were illuminated by small torches that were spaced out every fifty or so feet. It took nearly a minute for her eyes to adjust to the darkness around her. Her head was pounding, and she was still disoriented.

A pungent aroma of burning animal fat rose up into her nostrils, further awakening her to the surroundings. Looking first to her left and then to her right, she saw who or what it was that was carrying her.

The two hulking creatures were close to seven feet tall. Their morphologies and musculature were humanlike, but they were clearly not human. Hides as thick as rhinoceros, they were a dark-red in color with scaly snakelike patterns. The underside torso area was lighter in color with finer, thinner scales. They possessed what seemed to be a type of partial exoskeleton. External bones formed over the abdomen and two-to three-inch spikelike bones protruded from the shoulders and elbows. From her angle she wasn't able to see the bones that ran down the creatures' backs or the long prehensile tails with a bladed end.

They walked fully erect on powerfully built legs; however the leg bones were inverted below the knee like a satyr's. They had three clawed toes on each foot and three fingers and an opposable thumb on each hand.

Sprouting from their backs were massive batlike wings, each more than six feet in length. The tough leathery skin was stretched tight over the bony skeletal infrastructure. A network of veins was visible through the semitransparent membrane. An outer bone ran along the top of the wings. Although the bone naturally grew in flat, it had been manually filed to a razor's sharpness.

The creatures had large, rugged faces with reptilian eyes, broad, flat noses, and long pointed ears. Their mouths were lined with a set of twenty-four sharp teeth, including a pair of inch-long fangs at the top and two-and-one-half-inch mandibles at the bottom. They possessed thick black tendrils for hair, which they decorated with small pieces of bone. Protruding from the tops of each of their foreheads was a pair of thick, seven-to eight-inch-long horns.

The creatures wore leathery loincloths made from dried animal skins. The skulls of animals hung from their necks like trophies—foxes, badgers, rattlesnakes, and vultures.

"I must be in hell" was Tamiya's first thought, before logic and memories began to reassemble in her mind.

She remembered back to a half an hour earlier.

She and CJ had climbed up on a rocky ridge to try to get a better vantage point. She had been on the phone with Adam when, to her horror, four of the demonlike creatures swooped down from the sky.

Everything from there was a terrifying jumble.

Each of her captors held Tamiya by an arm, the toes of her shoes dragging along the ground. She saw that they were taking her toward an opening up ahead where the light was brighter.

As they entered a large chamber, she could hear the sound of conversation but couldn't understand a single word of the guttural sounding language being spoken. All conversation stopped as she was brought in.

The round chamber was approximately one hundred feet in diameter with a forty-foot arched ceiling. It was brightly lit by large torches and an eight-foot-wide fire pit. Although it had once been a natural formation, the chamber had been carved into an architectural work of art. The onyx granite floor had been polished to a glossy marblelike sheen. The curved ceiling had also been polished smooth. Bas-style reliefs had been sculpted into the walls. The reliefs were similar to the types of heroic battle sculpts lining the Parthenon or biblical scenes adorning medieval churches. However instead of angels, the "heroes" in the scenes looked like demons.

Just inside the chamber entrance, there were four more of the red-skinned males, two of which stood guard. There were also five of the creatures that were clearly female. The females stood a little taller than six feet and had either green-or purple-colored scaled skin. Their exoskeletal bones were lighter weight and their wings were smaller. Their faces were smooth and serpentine with large, almond-shaped eyes and high cheekbones. Three-inch horns protruded from their foreheads. They adorned their long tendril hair with colorful beads, bones, and feathers.

The females sat or reclined at the foot of an elaborate throne in the center of the chamber. The throne had literally been carved out of stone and embellished with intricately detailed decorative patterns and sculptures. There was a figure seated in the throne, but it was leaning back and almost completely in shadow.

There were also about a dozen smaller-sized creatures skittering about the chamber. Tamiya immediately saw their resemblance to the decomposing specimen that Loco Joe had in the formaldehyde jar. Standing between two feet and three feet in height, the scaly creatures were either brown, maroon, or dark-green in color. They had well-defined facial features, pointed ears, sharp fangs, and small horns. About half of them had wings.

The captors threw her down onto the cold granite floor at the foot of the throne. Tears welled in her eyes, and she trembled uncontrollably as she tried to make sense of what was happening. All around she could feel their probing reptilian eyes upon her, like a mammal in a pit of serpents.

"Please," she pleaded. "Oh god . . . please."

"Your . . . god . . ." came a voice from the figure seated on the throne, "has very little to do with us."

Tamiya looked up in surprise and shock when she heard English being spoken in an usual accent.

The creatures' tongues were thinner and longer than a human's. Because of this, there was a serpentine hissing sound to their voices.

The figure leaned forward into the light.

The blue-skinned male was a few inches shorter and more finely boned than the heavily armored red-skinned ones. His wings were neatly folded behind him, and his tail was casually draped over the arm of the throne. In some respects there was an almost aristocratic air about him. His nose was thinner, and his face was narrow with high cheekbones. His tendril-like hair was a pure-white in color, and his twin horns curved around like a ram's.

His blue reptilian eyes were fixed on Tamiya. She briefly noticed a flush of red appear along the sides of his face. Then it disappeared.

"What . . . what are you?" she gulped.

"What are we?" the creature asked, its voice serpentine. "Look into the recesses of your nightmares, human, and you will find us. Look into your history, your mythology, your religion. We are there too. Your kind has had many names for us, demons, goblins, the dark breed . . ." It stood to its full six-foot-seven-inch height. "We, human . . . are gargoyles."

"G-gargoyles?" Tamiya tried to process what she was hearing. "Like the statues on old churches?"

"Not myths. Not legends. From the time your Cro-Magnon ancestors began walking upright, we have been there. We were smaller then . . . weaker . . . easy to kill. When your kind learned of us, they hunted us to the brink of extinction. Our only way to survive and preserve our race was to adapt. We learned to hide and to enter our long sleep. Every five hundred years we emerged reborn—each time larger, stronger, smarter. But the humans were always there. And whenever you discovered us there would be war. Your ancestors, we knew them all. The Sumerians, the Babylonians, the Mayans, the Egyptians, the Greeks and Romans, even the medieval Europeans.

"When last we arose, five hundred years ago, once again your kind again nearly destroyed us. Only a precious few of our eggs had survived, and once again, we had to escape into our long sleep . . . and wait.

"I am V'Akiron. I was first awake." He spread his wings to their full fourteen-foot span as if to assert his power and majesty. "I carry within me, the memories of our race, our culture and language. Mine is to rule."

16

Five years ago, following a complex series of extremely gradual chemical reactions, the thick leathery outer layer of V'Akiron's thirteen-inch-tall egg had thinned and turned semitranslucent and brittle.

A clutch of 396 eggs had been buried a half mile deep in the cave several hundred years before. Of those, only twenty-four had survived—three thinkers, six warriors, eleven workers, and most valuably, three breeders.

V'Akiron was the first to awaken.

It took more than an hour for the twelve-pound, twenty-two-inch gargoyle to claw its way out of the gel-filled egg sac and be "born" into a new world. And then nearly a day and a half to climb 400 feet up out of the egg pit.

Over the next several months, the hatchling grew—surviving first on larvae, slugs, and insects, and later on lizards, rodents, and small game. Because of their unique physiology, gargoyles reached full maturity in approximately one year.

While the surviving spawn remained dormant in their eggs, V'Akiron ventured out—first from the confines of the cave and later into the world.

Like a vampire, he roamed by night and slept by day. Even at night he stuck to the shadows for fear of discovery. He wore long coats that would hide his wings and hats or hooded jackets to cover his rapidly growing horns.

Always skulking in dark alleyways or traversing the underground sewers systems, he moved through small towns and cities learning all that he could about this new world and the humans.

"For nearly a year, I walked among you," V'Akiron said. "Cloaked by the night, I learned of your ways, your culture, even your tongues. Je parle francaise. Ich spreche Deutsches. Я говорю на русском *Wǒ shuō zhōngguó huà*. Then I returned here to teach my awakening kindred and prepare them for the human world."

"I-I don't understand any of this," Tamiya said. "You say that a race of . . . of gargoyles has existed for thousands of years. There is absolutely nothing in the evolutionary genome that would—"

"We were a second species," the gargoyle lord simmered with rage. "We evolved along with you but apart . . . always apart. Whenever our two species came together, it led to war and death. Each time we emerged, we would find that humans had spread like a virus. You built cities and developed weapons and technologies. We were too few. Now if our kind is to survive, we need time to grow stronger and in number."

"But the world is different now," Tamiya said. "Five hundred years ago, yes, our ancestors were ignorant and superstitious. But now the discovery of another species wouldn't start a war. It would be front-page news."

"I know of your kind. You would be curious at first. Curiosity would become fear. Fear would become hatred. Hatred would become war."

"No. Clearly, you're a highly intelligent species." Tamiya took a step toward the blue-skinned gargoyle, trying to appeal to him. "My boyfriend is one of the most famous anthropologists in the world, he could—"

One of the female gargoyles sprung to her feet, hissing menacingly at Tamiya.

"Keep your place, S'Narra!" the gargoyle lord barked.

The female lowered her head submissively and drew back.

V'Akiron turned his attention back to Tamiya. "You are young for a human female?"

"Twenty-five," she replied.

"We grow quickly. I have lived only five years, but I carry the memories of thousands of years of my kind. Memories of life. Memories of wars. Memories of death."

Just then a powerfully deep, gravelly voice filled the chamber, speaking in the gargoyle language. All eyes turned to the huge gargoyle standing silhouette in the entrance to the chamber.

At seven feet, three inches, K'Urgoth was the tallest and most powerfully built of the red-scale skinned gargoyles. Like the others of his caste, he had an exoskeleton of thick bones, organic armor and shoulder and elbow bone spikes. His face was fierce and rugged, and he wore his tendril-like hair pulled into a kind of topknot. He had fourteen-inch long bull-like horns. His massive wings were lined with razor-sharp bone blades. Several skulls hung from the leather strap worn around his neck—a coyote, a mountain lion, an eagle, and . . . a human.

Tamiya was repulsed at the sight of the human skull. Then her eyes looked down to the three bowling-ball-sized objects dangling from the massive gargoyle's clawed hands.

The gargoyles tossed the objects into the chamber. They hit the floor with a dull, sickening splat, then rolled to a stop just a few feet from the throne. Tamiya recognized the severed heads of CJ, Shaggy, and Newt.

"No!" she shrieked. "Oh god no!"

With no one to acknowledge or comfort her, Tamiya could only sob over the loss of her friends.

K'Urgoth barely acknowledged the weeping human as he strode into the chamber. He spoke in the language of his ancestors as he knelt before the gargoyle lord.

"We have slain the human males, my lord" he reported.

The gargoyle language was replete with choppy words, hissing sounds, and short vowels.

V'Akiron could barely contain his fury. "Those were not my words!" he snarled.

K'Urgoth lowered his head further. "But . . . we were seen."

"Were you? Or did you only thirst for blood?"

K'Urgoth suppressed his smile. Soon the new trophies would be stripped, cleaned, and displayed. Like his ancestors, he had tasted human meat.

Knowing that it could risk their discovery, V'Akiron had forbade them from killing humans for hatred, food, or sport. There was more than enough game in the desert for the colony. With few exceptions, those orders were followed. However, the warriors were becoming restless and more difficult to control.

"Why?" Tamiya wailed. "Why did you have to kill them?"

K'Urgoth looked back at the annoying and insignificant human female. He could smell the sickly sweet aroma of her blood mingling with her salty tears and fear sweat. He gave only a growl.

"Take the human away," V'Akiron ordered.

The two red-skinned warrior gargoyles from earlier grabbed Tamiya by the arms.

"No, please, please let me go," she pleaded desperately.

Struggling and crying, Tamiya was dragged from the chamber.

V'Akiron sat back onto his elaborately carved stone throne, which was lined with gray and tan coyote pelts. Leaning on the armrest, he brought a hand up to his forehead, a gesture of fatigue and concern.

"You should kill the human creature now," K'Urgoth advised.

"It is not yours to decide," responded the gargoyle lord, not bothering to make eye contact.

The warrior inhaled. "The stench of it still lingers."

"You hate what you do not know."

"They are humans. What more is there to know?"

"It has been five hundred years since our kind flew among them."

"We should destroy them all. Now."

"That would only bring more."

"We have taken another female. The humans will seek them. They will come with their machines and weapons. Their colony is alone and isolated. There are only a few humans in number, many of them females and children. If we attack now—"

"I am first awake!" the gargoyle lord challenged, standing to face his taller and larger subordinate. "Mine is to decide for our kind. You, K'Urgoth, are second awake. Yours is only to lead the warriors! That is the way of things."

The warrior gargoyle lowered his head in deference.

"Yes, my lord."

V'Akiron placed a hand on the warrior's shoulder. "Be patient, brother. We must have time to grow in strength and in number."

17

"This is crazy!" Billy Lightfoot complained from behind the jail cell bars. "I've told y'all a hundred times what happened."

"Yeah right, giant man-bats took that girl," drawled LB.

Billy was in one of the two holding cells.

"I'm tellin' you, man, those things are out there."

"Quiet down," the sheriff called from inside his office. "I don't want to hear no more of your nonsense, Lightfoot."

The deputy got out from behind his desk and stood a few feet from across from the prisoner. "We've been lookin' for that girl since sunup and ain't found nothin', Billy. Every one of your worthless ass buddies that we talked to either had an alibi or swore up and down they didn't know anything."

"That's because they wasn't even there, like I told you."

"Somebody knows something. And you ain't helpin' by making up fairy tales."

"Look, dude, I know you've been tryin' to get back at us ever since you got that little tin badge. Just 'cuz we used to call you 'moosehead' back in high school—"

The deputy slammed his nightstick against the jail cell bars. "Keep mouthin' off, Billy, and I'll show you some things!"

Hearing the commotion, the sheriff rushed out of his office. "Goddammit, LB, go sit down and let me handle this," he ordered.

The deputy grudgingly went back over to his desk but refused to sit down.

The sheriff turned his attention back to Billy. "Now, Billy, you'd make it a heck of a lot easier on yourself if you was to just come clean right now. You think about this, if we find out that just one of your pack had something to do with that missing girl, you could be looking at conspiracy to a kidnapping. Because we are gonna find her, even if I have to cover every square inch of desert. And if she ain't alive, you're gonna find yourself charged with a whole lot worse."

Billy sat down on the small metal bunk and put his head in his hands. "What do you want me to say, sheriff? I've been telling you the truth since last night. Three of them things came and took that girl. I don't know where they came from or what they was—"

Just then a voice came from the front entrance. "I think I might," said Adam.

Everyone turned their attention to the front door.

A visibly shaken Adam walked into the station. His khaki shorts were covered with desert dust and sand, and his maroon shirt had two large sweat stains under the armpits.

"Where've you been, professor?" asked Sheriff McKain. "And what happened?"

"I haven't been completely honest with you, sheriff," Adam admitted.

The sheriff narrowed his eye. "Then maybe you better explain yourself."

Adam sat down in one of the chairs. He took a deep sigh, then looked the sheriff directly in the eyes.

"The truth is that . . . the old man, Loco Joe . . . he'd discovered a creature that bore a resemblance to what Billy described last night."

"I told ya!" Billy exclaimed. Then he looked over at LB. "Let me out of here, dummy."

The sheriff shot the young man a warning glance. Then he turned his attention back to Adam. "Do you care to explain to me how that fact just slipped your mind?"

Adam looked away in shame. "Yes . . . no. I mean, at the time we weren't sure exactly what the thing was. A hoax, some kind of mutation, who knows. We were going to take the specimen back to Berkeley for testing. Then, that night when Mr. Cunningham was killed . . . I didn't want it to be confiscated as possible evidence." He quickly added, "I know that was wrong."

"Mister, you were interfering with a homicide investigation and withholding evidence. For that I could lock you up right now."

"I apologize."

"And when those supposed bat-things took your student, you couldn't put two and two together?"

"Billy described their attackers as being seven feet tall with massive batwings. The specimen that Joe had discovered was less than three feet in length and didn't have wings."

"So if Loco Joe's little thing and Billy's man-bats are different, why do you all of a sudden believe Lightfoot now?"

"Because . . . clearly there is some similarity. And also because now my girlfriend and three more of my students are missing."

"What?" The sheriff stood up.

"Yes. And we've got to get back out there looking for them."

"Now hold on for a second. Out where? Where've you been?"

"We were about twelve miles northwest of here."

"Out in the badlands? What the hell where you doing out there?"

"We were able to track the GPS signal on Tegan's phone. But when we got there, all we found was the phone but no trace of her. We split up to see if we could find her. And that's when everyone else went missing."

"And you saw those giant bat things took 'em?"

"I didn't see them, but I heard. I was on the phone with Tamiya when something attacked them." Adam pulled out the blood-covered cell phone. "By the time I got to where they were, this is all I found."

The sheriff took the phone and turned it over in his hand, examining it.

"You know, professor, Loco Joe gettin' killed, your students disappearing, and now these wild tales about man-bats. So excuse me if I don't just roll over and take you at your word."

"Sheriff, it doesn't matter whether or not you believe me or even if you trust me. All I know is that I've got missing students, and we're losing time. So my question is, are you going to help me?"

The sheriff examined Adam's face, looking to see the truth in it. Without taking his eyes off Adam, he called to his deputy over his shoulder. "LB g'head and let Billy out of the cage."

"But dad," LB started to protest.

"I said let him out!"

Begrudgingly, LB opened the door to the cell and let Billy out.

"Thanks, moosehead," Billy insulted as LB glared at him.

"Okay, Billy, you say them man-bat things flew off with that girl?" asked the sheriff.

"Like I been tellin' you."

"What direction did they take her?"

"I don't know. It was dark."

"There's nearly a hundred miles of desert in every direction, boy, I'm gonna need some kinda bearing to start with."

"Wait a minute, what about your uncle?" Adam asked.

"Huh?" asked Billy. "What about him?"

"Remember the other day. He was chanting about demons returning to the mountains. Maybe he was referring to these creatures."

"My great uncle's ninety-two years old, half blind, and crazy as the day is long."

"Two Snakes?" The sheriff laughed. "That senile old Indian is almost as bad as Loco Joe."

"But maybe he knows something," Adam said. "We need to talk to him."

18

Tamiya was being roughly handled as she was led down the dimly lit corridor by two hulking gargoyles. Although they were no longer dragging her by the arms as before, the creatures walked less than a foot behind her. If she moved too slowly, one of the thick bodies would push up against her and shove her forward. One of them barked a harsh command in their language, which she took to mean that she was moving too slow. Resigned to the fact that she was a captive, Tamiya had begun to steel herself.

Up ahead she could see a brightening light.

Coming out of the corridor, they emerged into the main shaft. Tamiya's eyes widened in astonishment and disbelief.

The gargoyle's lair was a massive multichambered subterranean cavern branching off from a main shaft. Nearly one hundred feet in diameter and roughly three hundred feet deep, the cylindrical shaft was like an inverted 30-story building.

The scope and sophistication of the gargoyle's lair was astonishing. The illumination filling the shaft was produced by thousands of animal-fat-burning stone sconces built into the shear walls. Carved-in stairs ran along the interior walls of the shaft like a winding staircase. Dozens upon dozens of chambers of varying size had been manually hollowed out into the sides. She immediately recognized them to be habitats not unlike Indian cliff dwellings but larger and more complex.

It was a gargoyle city.

Dozens of the green-, red-, purple-, and blue-skinned gargoyles glided around the interior of the chamber like bats. There were also scores of the smaller gargoyles either flying about the shaft or climbing along the walls performing various functions.

Occupying the lowest rung of the colony's societal structure, the smaller worker caste gargoyles had evolved for specialized duties. They were the laborers, builders, small-game hunters, scavengers, gatherers, cooks, pelt skinners, leather tanners, clothes makers, artisans, caretakers, and servants. The creatures stood between two feet and three feet in height. Most were brown or tan in color and some had fur in addition to scales. While about one quarter of them had wings, most were wingless and flightless. There were four subspecies within the worker caste, each of which had adapted and evolved based upon their function within the colony. Already numbering more than five hundred, the workers were the most populous class of gargoyles in the colony.

Tamiya was still in a semiawestruck state when one of the gargoyles gruffly scooped her up in its arms. Before she could even protest, it had spread its wings and leapt off the overlook and into the shaft city.

The gargoyle flew out into the center of the shaft, then angled its body downward and began a slow spiraling descent.

As they flew downward, Tamiya opened her eyes to take it all in—in part out of sheer fascination and in part because she was trying to figure if there was a way for her to escape.

Although much of it was a blur, she was able to see into some of the individual habitats, which were lit from within. She saw what appeared to be living units. There was a chamber where worker gargoyles were stripping pelts and meat from various desert animals. One of the chambers was occupied by a half dozen of the red-skinned warrior gargoyles. Mounted on the walls of the chamber were various primitive, handmade bladed weapons and skull trophies.

Then, to her horror, she saw into the hatching chamber.

The chamber measured approximately 120 feet wide by fifty feet high by eighty feet deep. The entire back wall was a honeycomb-like structure with literally thousands hexagonal eighteen-by-eighteen-inch cells. Inside each cell was a round gargoyle egg. Through the semitranslucent leathery-skinned shell, she could see the shapes of fetal gargoyles. The egg room was being attended to by dozens of worker-caste gargoyles. Winged attendants flew along the honeycomb, identifying eggs that were ready to open. They would take those eggs from their cells and bring them to the "birthing nests." There were several six-by-six-foot, pelt-lined birthing nests, each capable of accommodating up to eight eggs. Flightless gargoyles attended to the nests. When the eggs tore open, thick gelatinous fluid would first spill out. Then a slime-covered, twelve-inch-to fourteen-inch-long gargoyle hatchlings would emerge.

"My god," Tamiya remarked to herself. "There are *thousands* of them."

As they neared the bottom of the shaft, she beheld one more sight that completely astonished her. Rising up from the floor of the shaft was a colossal seventy-foot-tall statue. Carved completely out of light-gray rock, the statue depicted a male and female gargoyle sculpted in a style reminiscent of a Michelangelo.

They flew around the massive, intricately detailed sculpture, then landed on a ledge beyond which was a small, cell-like chamber. The gargoyle forcibly shoved Tamiya into the chamber so hard that she fell to the dirt floor. Then it flew off.

Because the cell was carved directly into the side of the shaft, with an eighty-foot drop straight down to the stone floor, there was no concern that she would attempt to escape.

The chamber was sparse and small, measuring approximately twelve feet by twelve feet with an ten-foot high ceiling. The rock walls were rough and featureless. The meager illumination was provided by a single torch. There was a raised stone sleeping area lined with stitched-together rabbit pelts.

Just as Tamiya's eyes were adjusting to the darkness, she heard something that sounded like a moan.

She whipped around. "Who's there?" she asked, fear starting to grip her. "Is someone in here?"

The sound had come from behind the raised sleeping area. Tamiya took a timid step forward to look. She saw something huddled and shivering in the corner.

"Tegan?" Tamiya asked cautiously.

As Tamiya knelt down, the traumatized teen quickly backed away, cringing like a terrified deer. Her eyes were wide and wild, her hair stringy and tangled, and her face was covered with dirt and minor abrasions.

Tamiya held out an open hand in a calming manner. "Tegan, it's me."

Hysterically, Tegan began flailing her arms as if fighting off an attacker.

Tamiya managed to grab both of the terrified young girl's wrists. She pulled her close and held her tight. "Tegan! Tegan, it's me!" she said, rocking her gently. "Shhh, it's me."

Slowly, the teen began to calm and relax. Then the tears came.

19

"I told you they'd come back," the old Navajo said in his bone-dry voice.

Two Snakes had earned his name during his first hunting trip in the desert at seven years of age. In that outing the young brave had managed to kill not one but two large rattlers.

The ninety-two-year-old was now ancient. He had one good eye and a blind eye that was clouded over with cataracts. His weathered leathery skin was the color of raw umber and his long, snow-white hair was worn loose and free.

He was sitting in a handmade stick and leather strap rocking chair on the porch of his small, dusty clapboard house. Hanging dream catchers and wind chimes swayed in the breeze.

"Don't sound so crazy now, do I, nephew?" he asked with a chuckle.

A humbled Billy looked away from his uncle's one-eyed gaze.

"Just tell us what you know about these so-called bat things," said the sheriff impatiently.

"Please," Adam added. "It's important,"

Two Snakes sat back in his rocker. "The stories of the sky demons have been passed down by our people for hundreds of years. Only the last couple of generations have chosen not to listen," he said, looking over disapprovingly at Billy.

"The old ones say they came out of the ground like the cicada after a long cycle. They walked like men and flew on wings like bats. At first there were only a few, but before long, the sky grew black with their numbers. They killed many warriors taking their heads as prizes. At night, they would take our women. Then we learned to track them . . . to the mountains . . . to the caves.

"All the tribes came together to fight our common enemy—the Navajo, the Apache, the Hopi, the Paiute, even the Lakota and Yuma. All sent their braves from across the land to form the largest war party ever. Tens of thousands of warriors.

For many days, our ancestors fought the sky demons. Our arrows shot them out of the sky. We drove them back into the caves. We hunted them until there were no more."

Finished with his tale, Two Snakes gave a satisfied nod of his head.

Sheriff McKain was unimpressed. "So now I'm chasing ancient Navajo legends."

"These legends are true, sheriff. Ignore them if you want," warned Two Snakes. "But my ancestors told that one day the sky demons would return."

"Sheriff, you can't ignore this," said Adam. "We saw the carcass, and my students are missing."

"Okay, let's say I go along with this tall tale for the moment," the sheriff said to Two Snakes. "Where are these man-bats of yours supposed to be?"

Two Snakes pointed to the mountains in the far distance. "My people still call it the Demons Tower. The legends say the sky demons came up from the mountain caves, swarming like angry bees."

"Now you know ain't been nothin' in those mountains for years but dried-up mines and dusty old caves."

"Then doesn't that make sense that that would be the perfect place for them to hide?" asked Adam.

"About as much sense as the rest of this nonsense. Between his Indian myths and your cockamamie scientific specimen that you supposedly got from Loco Joe, that I ain't seen mind you, I'm s'posed to believe there's giant man-bats runnin' around out there."

"Sheriff, you can't—"

The sheriff held up a silencing hand. "I ain't ignoring it, professor. I got people missin' on my watch. Which means I gotta follow up any potential lead. So against my better judgment, I'm gonna take my deputies and check it out."

"Wait a minute, sheriff, the way he's telling it, there could be hundreds of those creatures in there. Don't you think you should call in the state police or the military or someone?"

"And tell them what?" The sheriff looked at Adam like he was crazy. "After they got through laughing their asses off, they'd probably haul *me* away."

"Sheriff, you—"

The sheriff cut him off again. "That don't mean I ain't gonna go in without backup. It'll just have ta be my own brand of backup."

* * *

An hour later the sheriff and his deputies were back at Charlie's Diner. The sheriff was at the center table and more than forty of the local townies had crowded into the small diner and gathered around.

"All right, boys," the sheriff said, "as of right now, I'm officially deputizing each and every one of you."

"What's going on, sheriff?" asked Otis.

"Yeah, what's this all about?" echoed Slim.

"I'll let y'all know in a few. Right now, as my deputies, I will be grantin' you temporary authorization to go into your personal weapons stashes, both legal and illegal. I know you got 'em so don't hold back. I'm givin' you permission to pull 'em out and my personal guarantee that nothing, no matter how big or small, will be confiscated."

Several of the locals looked at one another excitedly.

"Anything, sheriff?" asked Carl Junior.

"Whatever you got, Carl."

"Well, all right then."

"Now I want all of you to grab up your weapons, hop into your vehicles, and meet me at the edge of town in exactly thirty minutes. You'll get your official briefing then."

20

Tegan huddled trembling in the corner of the small, dank stone room, her knees drawn up protectively to her chest. Nearby, there was a discarded small animal limb that had been skinned and tossed in as food. A nauseating stench of vomit lingered in the cave from when the teen had thrown up earlier.

Tamiya put her hands on both sides of Tegan's face and looked into her shell-shocked eyes. "Tegan, you have to focus," she said. "Eyes on me! Eyes on me."

Slowly, recognition began to appear in Tegan's eyes.

"Tam-Tamiya?" she asked meekly.

"Yes, it's me. Thank god, I found you. We thought that gas station attendant had taken you."

"Billy? No, he tried to save me. It was those things!" She was starting to lose it again. "They took me, and they . . . they . . ."

"It's okay. I'm here now."

"What are those things, Tamiya? Are they some kind of devils?"

"No, they're gargoyles."

"Gargoyles?"

"They're a kind of undiscovered species," she looked around. "We're inside their lair."

"What about the others? Professor Landis, CJ . . . They'll come for us, right?"

"I don't know about Adam, but the boys . . . they didn't . . ."

Realizing what she was being told, Tegan's eyes widened. "No, no," she shook her head in denial.

"But listen, Yeardley stayed behind to tell the sheriff. They'll have to believe her."

"But they won't know where to look. We flew for miles. Nobody'll ever find us. Tamiya, I don't want to die!"

Just then a gargoyle landed on the ledge outside the chamber.

The green-skinned, six-foot-three-inch female looked like a reptilian Amazon. Her body was shapely, seductive, and well muscled. Like all females, her wings were smaller than the males but still more than capable of flight. Her golden-yellow reptilian eyes were almost catlike. Her long, raven-black hair tentacles cascaded down past her shoulders and partially covered her naked breasts. A short, leather loincloth was wrapped tightly around her hips.

Upon seeing the gargoyle, Tegan curled up in fear.

Tamiya recognized the female from earlier in the large chamber. She stood to face the taller female. "Why are you keeping us here? What do you want from us?"

S'Narra seemed to ignore the questions. She extended her long, clawed fingers and slowly raked them across the human's face.

"Sssoft," the female gargoyle said with a slight hiss to her voice. With a flick, her sharp claw sliced an inch-long cut along Tamiya's cheek, drawing blood.

The gargoyle brought the claw to her mouth. Her thin tongue darted out and licked the droplets of blood with a smile. "Warm. Sweet blood."

Tamiya drew back.

S'Narra smiled, then walked around to Tamiya as if taking measure of her.

She grabbed Tamiya by the chin and drew her face close. "You humans are fragile creatures."

Tamiya said nothing.

S'Narra's eyes probed her curiously. "He is drawn to you, you know. The coloring . . . when the males are aroused, they cannot hide it."

"What?" Tamiya asked.

"V'Akiron."

"You mean the blue one? Your king?"

"He is our lord."

"And you're his . . . his queen?"

S'Narra laughed. "I am not a breeder. I am . . . no word in your language . . . I am first of seven."

"You mean like a harem?"

"What is harem?"

"It means that he has several females."

S'Narra smiled. "It is said our males would sometimes take human females. Mate with them . . ."

Tamiya turned away in disgust.

"You wish to leave?" S'Narra asked.

"Yes." Tamiya's eyes grew wide with hope.

"You will never leave. Be happy you are not food?"

"F-food?" Tegan's trembling sob came from the dark corner.

"But no one is to touch you," S'Narra reluctantly assured. "He has given the word."

"What do you want from us?" Tamiya asked.

"There is a war coming."

"But why? You don't understand . . ."

"No! It is you who do not understand. Fear . . . hatred. As old as time. It is born in the blood of humans. It is born in the blood of gargoyles. Just as we are your demons, human . . . you are ours."

21

It was just after three in the afternoon.

The two sheriff's cruisers sat just on the outskirts of town where the edge of the desert began. Gathered before them were more than thirty assorted vehicles—cars, light trucks, ATVs, jeeps, Otis's tractor trailer, and Slim's tanker truck. The ragtag collection of locals who had come out wore getups ranging from jeans and t-shirts, to green and khaki camouflage paramilitary attire. People were armed with everything from knives, shotguns, and rifles to custom-made and authentic military surplus weapons. There were several fully automatic assault weapons, a portable rocket launcher, and even a Jeep-mounted anti-aircraft gun.

The sheriff looked over his assembled posse with pride.

"Impressive group, ain't they?" he boasted to Adam who was standing beside him. "Armed to the teeth, and there's a good amount of military experience represented out there as well. But that ain't the all of it. I've also ordered in air support."

"Air support?"

The sheriff pointed out to the two helicopters in the distance that were flying toward them like a pair of giant insects. As they came closer, Adam could see that one of the choppers was dark maroon and the other was a cobalt blue. Painted on the side of each was the yellow Red Rock Helicopter Tours logo. Both choppers had been modified to carry twin miniguns.

"Meet the Olsen Twins," the sheriff said as the choppers gracefully landed on either side of the assembly of vehicle.

Larry and Barry Olsen were the best chopper pilots in the state. After serving tours in Iraq and Afghanistan a decade before, the brothers had come home and opened their helicopter tours business. Though they were identical twins, the brothers had strikingly different appearances. Baseball-cap-wearing Larry was heavyset with a thick red tangled beard, long hair pulled back in a ponytail, and numerous tattoos. Barry was of normal build, clean-shaven, and wore his hair short.

The sheriff held up a bullhorn. "All right, everyone settle down," he said. "First up, thank you boys . . ."—he spotted a couple of women in the group—"and girls for comin' out. Now you've all been brought up to speed on what we're supposed to be up against as best we can tell."

"Yeah, them giant bat man-things!" Slim yelled out.

"That's right. Now before everybody goes off and gets all excited whoopin' and hollerin', keep in mind, this is based on a piece of roadkill discovered by Loco Joe and the ramblings of a half-blind ninety-two-year-old Indian. We might just as easily find some lost college students suffering from exposure and hallucinations.

"Bottom line is this is a rescue mission first, and not everybody running around lookin' for monsters. Now in addition to your standard shotguns, rifles, and handguns, I've let you all go into your stashes and pull out the heavy artillery—M-16s, TEC-9s, grenades, you name it. But this is a one-time thing. After today, I don't want to see as much as a shell casing from an illegal firearm in my town, you got me?"

Carl Junior held up his portable rocket launcher. On the side of the army-green-colored weapon was a painting of a 1940s-style pinup model and a name "Suzy" in cursive type.

"Don't worry, sheriff," he said. "I only break Suzy out for special occasions."

There was laughter from the crowd.

"Now I know this is the kind of action you folks have just been itchin' for. Ground rules: This is a police operation, which means you follow a chain of command that starts and stops with me. Nobody fires so much as a spitball unless I say. Are we clear?"

There were assorted nods of agreement.

"Are we *clear*?" he repeated with more emphasis.

A collective response went up. "Yes, sir, sheriff!"

Just then, there was the roar of motorcycle engines. Six brightly colored motocross bikes snaked their way through the vehicles. The lead biker rode up and stopped in front of the sheriff.

The sheriff looked at Billy. "I figured after I cut you loose you and your renegades would hightail it in the other direction."

"Some of us decided to join the party."

"And you ain't scared, Billy? After all you supposedly saw some of them things."

"I did. But we figured there might be some kinda reward in rescuin' them college folks." Billy then looked the sheriff directly in the eyes. "Plus I wanna see the look on all your faces when you realize I wasn't lyin'."

"Fair enough. You, boys, got your guns?"

"Most of us. I ain't too much into guns myself," Billy reached behind his neck and slid the crossbow from the case strapped to his back. "But I didn't come unarmed."

"A god-blessed crossbow? Son, look at all the firepower around here, and you show up with a pea shooter."

"My weapon of choice."

"Suit yourself."

The sheriff held the bullhorn back up to his mouth.

"All right, people, let's move it out!" he ordered.

Engines started up. Rotor blades turned.

Three hunting buddies dressed in camouflage fatigues, Shane, Luke, and Dusty, got into their green pickup.

"You think them man-bat things is really out there?" Shane asked.

Luke held up his pump action 30-06 caliber shotgun. "Don't know, but if they is, I'm gonna mount one of 'em's head right over my fireplace."

"Mount hell," said Dusty. "I'm gonna git me one alive and sell it to the *National Enquirer*. How much you think something like that'd be worth? I'm guessin' about a million dollars?"

The three laughed.

22

V'Akiron was seated on his throne, his mind heavy in thought. K'Urgoth burst into the main chamber and walked past the guards.

The gargoyle lord stood. "What is your meaning?"

The warrior gargoyle knelt. "The humans. They are approaching."

V'Akiron narrowed his eyes. "Gather your warriors."

23

A swirling cloud of desert dust trailed behind the convoy of cars, trucks, and motorcycles closing in on the Demon's Tower. The sheriff's cruiser was out in the lead.

Inside of the vehicle, the sheriff was calling out orders as he coordinated the posse. Adam sat in the passenger seat beside him.

"You should know I don't like being played the fool, professor," the sheriff warned him.

"That's not my intention," Adam assured.

"Well, you just better hope this all don't turn out to be some kinda joke."

"You know everything I do."

"You don't have much of a track record for the truth with me, now do you?"

"We had no idea about the carcass."

"But how about after your student got carried off, and you heard the Lightfoot boy's story? You're an educated man. You're tellin' me you couldn't put two and two together?"

Adam started to say something to defend himself, but the sheriff cut him off.

"Instead, you decided to suppress information that could have aided in my investigation. Now look at where that got you. If these things is real . . ." He shook his head, refusing to give the absurd idea any credence. "But, on the other hand if you, Billy, and old Two Snakes have got me tyin' up time and manpower on some wild-goose chase, I'm gonna be personally chargin' somebody with something."

"Sheriff, my girlfriend and students are out there."

"Maybe if you'd have said something in the first place, they wouldn't be."

* * *

Nearly sixty of the warrior class gargoyles were assembling atop the rock tower that overlooked the flat desert basin below. The tall heavily built creatures had varying appearances, and many sported facial markings and skin patterns that resembled natural tattoos.

Below they could see the mechanical specks approaching at a high rate of speed.

"Humans," K'Urgoth said with disdain. "I can smell their stench from here."

"They will have weapons," said the warrior gargoyles to his left. He was bald, horned, and had a jagged six-inch-long scar slashed across the right side of his face. It was a souvenir from the mountain lion whose skull now hung around his neck.

"They are weak."

* * *

As the caravan came to within a quarter of a mile of the tower, the sheriff ordered everyone to slow down.

"We need to approach with caution," the sheriff said over his microphone. The transmission was picked up by the 2-way radios in the other vehicles.

"All right, professor," he said to Adam, "looks pretty quiet to me. Where are these things of yours supposed to be?"

"I don't know," Adam said.

"Like I said, we'd better not be on some—"

At that moment, the sheriff noticed the small dots rising up in the air from atop the tower. From that distance, they looked like bats exiting a cave.

He squinted his eyes behind his sunglasses. "What the hell?"

"Sheriff, you seein' this?" asked a voice over the crackling radio.

"Everybody stay calm and follow my commands."

As the convoy continued moving forward, the figures grew in both size and detail. Within a couple of minutes, the humans were able to make out what creatures flying toward them in formation looked like.

"God in heaven," the sheriff remarked in disbelief.

"Son-of-a-bitch!" someone said over the radio.

"Lookit them things!" came another voice.

"Everybody cut the chatter," the sheriff ordered.

"Sheriff, maybe we should turn back," Adam suggested. He was calculating the massive size of the creatures.

"Turn back? You was the one that got us out here!"

"There are at least fifty or sixty of them. We might not be well-enough prepared."

"Are you crazy? You've seen the firepower my folks're carrying."

The sheriff flipped a switch that activated the bullhorn speaker on the top of his cruiser.

"People, we got incoming," he announced.

Cars began swerving to a stop. Townspeople began exiting their vehicles, bringing their weapons with them—handguns, rifles, shotguns, machine guns. The gargoyles carried bone knives, axes, clubs, spears, and other primitively fashioned weapons. The mismatch was almost laughable.

Initially shocked by the appearance of the creatures that looked like the stuff of nightmares, the sheriff composed himself and reasserted his authority.

"Hold for my orders!" he instructed.

With the gargoyles eight hundred feet away and closing, the townspeople crouched behind their cars and open doors for cover. Rounds were chambered. Weapons were cocked and ready. Everyone was tense and focused although there were a few who were starting to become unnerved.

The sheriff held up his hand like an official about to signal the start of a race. "Steady!" he ordered.

The gargoyles were six hundred feet away.

"Steady!"

Four hundred feet.

"Steady!"

Two hundred feet.

The sheriff brought down his hand and gave the order. "Open fire!"

Immediately, dozens of weapons sprung to life. Gunfire was erupting everywhere—automatic weapons, shotguns, handguns. The noise was near deafening.

At that same instance, K'Urgoth barked out a command, and the gargoyles broke formation. The creatures were surprisingly fast and agile, executing barrel rolls and sharp turns that moved them out of the line of fire.

While there were rounds from that first volley that were able to find their targets and cause damage, only five of the gargoyles were hit—one fatally, one seriously, and three superficially. The higher-caliber rounds were able to penetrate the creature's rhinoceros-hard hides; other bullets simply bounced off the gargoyle's steel-hard exoskeleton bone plates.

"Goddamn, them things is tough!" someone yelled.

The gargoyles began circling back around, increasing velocity as they launched an attack.

The creatures were moving much faster this time, zigging and zagging to make themselves more difficult targets.

"Get down!" Sheriff McCain ordered as he pushed the unarmed Adam to the ground beside the cruiser. "Stay there!"

An assault wave of gargoyle swooped into the confused humans. Using the razor-sharp bone blades lining their wings, the gargoyles decapitated two people and cleaved another literally in half at the waist.

The swift, brutal, and bloody slayings of their friends horrified the townies. In truth, no one in the posse had been prepared for this. There were only two or three people who even thought that the creatures might be real. Some simply came out of curiosity, expecting to get a gander the latest Chupacabra or Jersey Devil sighting. Others couldn't resist an opportunity to break out their weapons, hoping that the sheriff might let them fire off some rounds. They'd expected to drive around for a while, wait while the sheriff and deputies checked out the caves. Then afterward they'd crank up their stereos, crack open some beers, and fire up their portable grills for a big, raucous tailgating party. Instead they were now in a desperate fight for their lives.

A wave of gargoyles swooped in from the right side, slashing people with axes, bludgeoning them with clubs, and impaling them with spears. Screams, confusion, and fear spread through the posse ranks like wildfire, and all semblance of discipline broke down. People were running and shooting in all directions.

Terrified, Dusty was frantically flooring his pickup truck, which was fishtailing as it spat up sand and rock trying to negotiate its escape. Shane and Luke were standing in the back of the truck, firing the bed-mounted anti-aircraft gun at three gargoyles swooping in from behind. One of the gargoyles was hit square in the chest, but another slammed into both men knocking them out of the vehicle. The third clamped to the side of the truck, tore off the door, and yanked a screaming Dusty out of the cab. Like pack hunters, several of the gargoyles descended upon the men, bludgeoning them with clubs and axes and tearing them apart.

Otis had climbed up the ladder to the top of his rig and was firing off an AK-47. "C'mon, you bat-demon-looking sons-o'-bitches, taste some of this!"

He hit one of the gargoyles in the wing, tearing a three-inch hole in the membrane. The slightly injured creature changed trajectory, flew a half circle, and decapitated the big man, hat and all.

Slim saw the headless body of his best friend sink to its knees then tumble off the top of the tractor trailer.

"Otis! Otis!" Slim called out.

As Slim ran toward the truck, a gargoyle swooped down and grabbed the wiry man by the shoulders with its foot claws. Its prey secured, the gargoyle changed direction and flew straight up in the air, rising 150 feet. The creature released its grip, letting the screaming human fall. Slim slammed into the ground with a thud accompanied by the sound of breaking bones. He didn't move after that.

The chopper being flown by Larry Olsen was chasing a gargoyle, firing at it like in a dogfight.

"Hold still, goddammit!" he said through clenched teeth.

He looked up to see another gargoyle headed directly for him in a kamikaze attack. The creature crashed through the window and into the cockpit. The chopper exploded a second later.

Two gargoyles had latched onto either side of Barry Olsen's chopper and were clawing into the metal. The chopper began spinning around out of control as it lost altitude.

"Mayday! Mayday! Mayday!" Barry frantically called into his radio microphone.

Both gargoyles leapt off the chopper less than twenty feet from the ground. It crashed to the desert floor, tumbled end over end for two hundred feet, then burst into flames.

Wally was firing his pump action shotgun. A gargoyle flew up and hovered about thirty feet away, keeping aloft by its flapping wings. The creature flung a five-foot-long spear, impaling the deputy through the chest.

Panicked townspeople were trying to start up their vehicles and flee the scene of carnage, which made them only more obvious targets as gargoyles landed on cars, smashed windows, and pulled out drivers and passengers. Others tried to run away, but they were like rabbits trying to flee hunting falcons. The men and women were quickly, brutally, and mercilessly snatched up, each time screaming and flailing like helpless prey.

The sheriff was standing up in the middle of the mayhem, firing in all directions.

"Sheriff, we have to get out of here!" Adam called out. "They're killing everyone!"

"Just keep down, professor!" the sheriff ordered.

The sheriff looked around frantically for his youngest deputy. "Where's LB?" he asked. "Where's my boy!"

Then he spotted the unmoving body of his son lying facedown about fifty feet away.

24

"C'mon!" Billy yelled to his friends as he kick-started his bike. "We gotta get outta here!"

Four of the motorcycles broke off from the main fighting. The other two had already fallen.

The bikes took off, heading away at top speed. Two gargoyles saw the fleeing bikers and veered off after them.

The bikes sped across the sand and headed to an area with more rugged terrain. There were rock formations that rose up and jutted out, trees that provided cover, as well as cliffs and ravines. The bikers wanted to make it as difficult as possible for the gargoyles to chase them. The four extreme bikers rode like daredevils—turning, jumping, darting, evading.

But the gargoyles, flying roughly thirty feet above, matched the bikers turn for turn.

Realizing that the tactic wasn't working, Billy called back, "Gotta lose 'em! Split up!"

The bikes split into two groups. One gargoyle went after the two bikes fleeing to the left, the other went after Billy and another rider.

Alchise "Al" Blackcloud and his younger brother Chatto headed for the low ground.

At sixteen years old, Chatto was the second youngest member of the Renegades, having joined the group only two months prior. In celebration, he had convinced is hairstylist big sister to shave his long hair into a Mohawk and give him a multicolor dye job. While he was a good rider, he was inexperienced and had a smaller, relatively underpowered Kawasaki X125. That made him the easier target. The pursuing gargoyle swooped in and plucked the teenaged Apache off the orange-and-black motocross bike and, in one fluid motion, flung him into a rock wall. Chatto's screams were silenced on impact.

"Chatto! Chatto!" Alchise howled in horror as he witnessed the sudden and violent death of this younger brother.

Putting his foot out for balance, he quickly whipped around his powerful Kawasaki X450. Both shocked and enraged, Alchise pointed the yellow and black tiger-striped bike directly at the oncoming gargoyle.

The gargoyle had already set its sights on the second brother. Fighting back tears, Alchise gritted his teeth and opened up the throttle to full. Releasing the handbrake, he headed straight for the creature.

As if playing a game of chicken, the nineteen-year-old and the gargoyle sped directly toward one another. Alchise screamed in hatred and anguish.

They collided.

The motocross bike continued out from under Alchise as the larger heavier gargoyle knocked him back. As momentum continued to carry them, the creature clamped its claws into the teen's shirt and chest. With a powerful swoop of its wings, the gargoyle began gaining altitude, and within seconds, they were two hundred feet in the air.

"You killed my little brother you son of a demon bitch!" Alchise ranted delirious with grief, fear, and fury.

Instead of trying to pry himself away from the gargoyle, Alchise hooked his right arm underneath the creature's armpit in a kind of a wrestling hammerlock. The gargoyle realized what was happening all too late. With his free hand, Alchise reached down and unsheathed the large Bowie knife strapped to his leg. The young Apache's scream sounded like a war cry as he plunged the ten-inch blade into the creature's chest.

The gargoyle howled in pain as the blade tore through its tough hide, severing a major artery. Alchise withdrew the blade, and bright cerulean-colored blood spewed out from the creature's gaping wound. The gargoyle's defense reflexes immediately kicked in as it tried to throw off the victim that had suddenly become an attacker. Alchise only tightened his grip. He plunged the knife into the gargoyle's neck up to the hilt, opening a deep gash. The creature emitted a bloodcurdling, high-pitched screech.

Wings flailing, the gargoyle bucked like a rodeo bull. Teeth gritted and eyes intense, Alchise held fast and pressed the attack. He picked out vulnerable spots, stabbing at the neck, eyes, and ears. The blade slashed open the gargoyle's throat, gouged out an eye, and tore through an eardrum.

As gargoyle and human were locked in a death struggle more than two hundred feet in the air, the creature's blue blood mingled with Alchise's red.

Its wings no longer responding, the gravely wounded gargoyle spun out of control and headed back to earth. As the pair fell, Alchise maneuvered around to the creature's back as if he were mounting a horse. He was still crazed with bloodlust and continued stabbing viciously. Plummeting to the ground, the Apache rode the shrieking gargoyle all the way down as they crashed through a thicket of tree branches then onto the rock-hard desert floor.

* * *

Billy and Tommy "Howler" Anders had split off to the right taking the higher ground. They had been followed by the second gargoyle.

Twenty-year-old Howler had been Billy's best friend since the third grade. He was five foot ten inches tall with an athletic build. He had recently taken to wearing his long sandy blond hair in "whiteboy" dreadlocks.

"Billy, it's catchin' up!" Howler frantically reported.

Billy looked over his shoulder and saw the ferocious red-skinned gargoyle closing in on them, its yellow eyes filled with fury. The two riders hunched down on their bikes, trying to coax out any extra speed they could.

"C'mon, Howler, ride!" Billy shouted.

Howler tried to zigzag his red-and-gold Suzuki, but the predatory gargoyle matched the maneuver. It was flying less than thirty feet behind.

"I can't shake it, man!" Howler exclaimed.

"Lead it left!" Billy shouted. He reached over his shoulder to the case strapped to his back and pulled out the crossbow. A bolt was already preloaded.

Still racing at more than forty miles an hour, he turned in the seat of the bike and aimed behind him.

"Down!" Billy yelled to Howler.

Howler ducked, and Billy fired.

The steel bolt sailed right past the gargoyle, narrowly missing it.

"Dammit!" Billy cursed.

Both bikes poured on speed as the furious gargoyle intensified its pursuit. Billy pulled up, and the two were riding side by side.

Howler chanced a quick look back. "It's comin' in again!"

Billy looked at the terrain around them. Then up ahead at the overlook.

He pointed up ahead. "Pour it on, dude, then when I give the word, brake!"

"But—," Howler started.

"Just do it, man!

The gargoyle was closing fast. Twenty-five feet. Twenty. Fifteen. Ten. Five.

"Brake and duck!" Billy yelled.

The two bikes went into simultaneous skids, dust kicking up all around them. They partially laid down their bikes.

The surprised gargoyle overshot them as momentum continued to carry it. It spread its wings wide to slow, then started twisting to correct itself.

Everything seemed to move in slow motion. Billy raised his crossbow, took aim, and fired.

The bolt went right into the gargoyle's neck and through its throat. Furiously the creature clawed at the bolt trying to pull it out. Its wings drooped as it lost altitude like a broken kite, finally falling to the ground.

As the gargoyle lay on the ground convulsing and gurgling, light-bluish-colored foam filled its mouth.

Billy and Howler ran up to the creature that was shuddering and gagging.

Eyes wide with fury, Howler looked around until he spotted a football-sized bolder. He picked up the thirty-pound stone, stood straddle over the gargoyle, and brought it down hard on the creature's head. He smashed it down three more times, caving the gargoyle's head in until it didn't move any longer.

It took a few seconds for Howler to calm down from the adrenaline, fear, and anger that had been coursing through his body. He stood over the dead creature, still breathing heavily.

Billy went over and picked up his bike.

"Where you goin'?" Howler asked.

"Back," Billy replied.

"Whoa, whoa, whoa! Are you crazy? Did you see how many of those things there were!"

"We gotta try."

* * *

Several minutes later, Billy and Howler made it back to the site of the battle. They stopped roughly a hundred yards away, set down their bikes, and crouched behind several large boulders.

When they looked out, they were horrified.

The scene was a massacre.

Most of the townies were already dead. A few of the wounded were crawling around on their hands and knees in pain and disorientation, blood covering their bodies. Only five people were still standing, hopelessly trying to fight back.

Gargoyles circled the remaining survivors like vultures. Every few seconds, one would swoop in and pluck up a victim, whose screams would then fill the air.

"Jeezus, they're getting slaughtered," Howler said.

Billy pulled out his crossbow.

Howler pushed his arm down, stopping him. "Dude, they're already dead."

The sheriff was the last man standing. He had run out of rifle ammo and tossed the weapon aside. He pulled out his service revolvers. Holding a Colt in each hand, he alternated firing left and right.

BLAM, BLAM.

Adam was still lying on the ground beside the sheriff's cruiser.

"Take the car, professor!" the sheriff shouted. "I'll try and keep 'em off you."

BLAM, BLAM.

"What about you?" Adam asked.

"Just get out of here. You can reach state police on the radio, tell 'em what we're up against."

BLAM, BLAM.

The sheriff looked down at Adam. "Sorry I didn't believe you, professor. I'm sorry I—"

Just then the blade end of a gargoyle's tail tore through the sheriff's abdomen. When the blood-coated blade was withdrawn, the lawman fell to the ground. K'Urgoth was revealed to be standing behind him.

Adam looked up in absolute terror, not just at the massive gargoyle, but at seeing the dozens of other gargoyles landing behind it.

It was over.

K'Urgoth walked up and stood over Adam. The gargoyle reached down and grabbed Adam around the neck, its massive clawed hand nearly encircling it. With one hand, K'Urgoth effortlessly held Adam up off the ground.

Adam closed his eyes and awaited his fate. Instead the gargoyle studied the college professor with both curiosity and disgust. It pulled Adam to within inches of its face.

"I can smell the female on you," K'Urgoth said in a voice that sounded like cracking bones.

Adam's eyes opened in surprise, both at hearing the creature speak and of the reference to the "female."

"T-Tamiya?" he choked.

"You are the human she called A-dam?"

"Y-yes."

Sneering, the warrior opened his hand dropping Adam to the ground.

Adam staggered to his feet. There were more than two dozen gargoyles now surrounding him. All around the bodies of dead townspeople littered the ground.

"I would kill you now, human, and take your head" K'Urgoth declared, "but V'Akiron has given the word."

K'Urgoth looked to the gargoyle standing to Adam's right.

"L'Orok!" he ordered.

The bald, scar-faced gargoyle slammed its fist into Adam's temple, knocking the college professor unconscious.

25

Billy and Howler remained out of sight behind the grouping of boulders. The carnage from the one-sided battle had left both young men in a state of near shock. A hundred yards away were the dead bodies of their friends and neighbors, and smashed and burned out vehicles that were still smoldering.

They saw two of the creatures picking up the college professor, who looked to be unconscious. They took to the sky heading back to Demon's Tower. Several of the other creatures were collecting their dead, which they also flew away. A few could be seen picking through the humans. They would kneel down and lop off heads using sharpened bone knives.

"Oh my god, oh my god, oh my god," muttered Howler. "This is like some kind of a nightmare, man what are we gonna do now?"

"We gotta try to get back into town," said Billy. "Warn everybody and then call for help."

"With them things flying around? They'll grab us before we get a hundred feet."

"It'll be dark in a couple of hours. We'll wait until then."

Howler noticed the huge gargoyle in the middle pointing instructions to the others.

"Wait a minute, Billy," he said. "Look."

The large gargoyle flew into the air, followed by twenty others. The group began flying in a southerly direction.

"Oh no," Billy said.

"What?" asked Howler.

"Do you see the direction they're flying in?"

Howler's eyes followed the creatures, "They look like they're heading southwest." Then he put it together. "Oh man, they're headed to Redbone."

26

Adam's eyes slowly opened.

His head was throbbing, and he felt sharp, stinging pain from the nasty cut just below his temple. He was in some kind of a cold, dimly lit room, but the walls looked to be solid rock.

For a second he imagined he heard Tamiya's voice.

"Adam?" Tamiya's voice said again.

That brought him almost completely out of his fog. "Tam?"

"Yes," she confirmed.

"Tam! Thank god." He tried to sit up, and a jolt of electric pain went through his head.

"Don't try to get up," Tamiya put her hand on his chest. "You might have a concussion."

Adam was lying on the raised sleeping area in a bed of animal pelts. Tamiya was sitting on the edge beside him.

"Where-where are we?"

"For lack of a better description, we're in their lair. They brought you in here a couple of hours ago."

Adam noticed that one of Tamiya's shirtsleeves was torn off. She held up the wadded up, bloodstained piece of material "I was able to stop the bleeding for now," she explained.

"Head hurts."

"What happened out there? I could hear what sounded like gunfire and explosions."

"It was a nightmare. The sheriff . . . some of the people from town. After we figured out where you were, we tried to mount a rescue. We had no idea. There were dozens of them. The creatures slaughtered everyone."

Then Adam spotted Tegan huddled in the corner. Her knees were pulled tightly to her chest, and she was incoherently rocking back and forth.

"Tegan!" he said. "You found her! Is she okay?"

"She's pretty traumatized,"

Adam looked around hopefully. "What about the boys, where are they?"

"The gargoyles . . . they-they killed them."

Adam's face filled with pain, and he closed his eyes shaking his head. "No."

Tears began welling in Tamiya's eyes. "It's like a horrible dream. I keep praying I'll wake up."

"These creatures. You called them . . . gargoyles?"

"That's what they are."

"You're saying that they're gargoyles . . . real gargoyles?"

"Yes. The same creatures that have been depicted in gothic architecture, in myths, in temple carvings for thousands of years. I know it sounds crazy, but I've seen them. Talked to them."

"They spoke in English," Adam recalled. "I thought I'd imagined it."

"According to their leader or whatever he is, they're a hidden species that has existed for thousands of years. Dying out and reemerging every few hundred years. Think about it, Adam, it makes sense. The medieval Europeans, the Greeks and Romans, the Aztecs, the ancient Egyptians, even earlier . . . all those cultures have stories or art depicting winged demons. Those myths must have been rooted in fact."

Adam shook his head, trying to make sense of it. "You're telling me these creatures . . . these gargoyles . . . date back to before ancient Egyptian civilization and somehow we've never seen them?"

"They're able to go into a kind of hibernation period that lasts about five hundred years. It's probably some kind of a defense mechanism to preserve their species. I don't know the science behind it. That's why they only show up at certain times in human history. Apparently the last time this happened was during the middle ages, sometime in the 1500s. They were nearly wiped out then, but they were able to hide some of their eggs and put them into hibernation."

"What else have you found out?"

"I've only been able to fill in bits and pieces of the genetic puzzle. They appear to be a kind of reptilian mammalian hybrid. Cold-blooded and highly evolved. From what I've seen, there appear to be three categories, which I'd classify as worker, warrior, and thinker—divided into a caste system. The workers are the small ones, no more than three feet in height. They seem adapted to perform specialized tasks—servants, builders, laborers. The carcass Loco Joe found was one of the workers.

"The hunter/warriors are the big red ones. They're very strong and deadly.

"Then the last ones are what I call the thinkers. Blue-skinned, highly intelligent. They're closer to humans in size and build. I only saw a couple of them. My guess is they are the ruling caste."

"So these creatures could have evolved on a parallel path."

"You're the anthropologist. But what I've observed is that they have comparable cranial size and capacity. They're not animals Adam. They're more intelligent than reptiles . . . more intelligent than primates . . . they're as intelligent as we are."

Adam let the sobering information sink in. "How many are in here?" he asked.

She shook her head. "I don't know . . . hundreds at least . . . maybe even a thousand. Most of those being the smaller workers. But that's not even the worst of it."

"What do you mean?"

She took a second. "They're breeding."

"Breeding?"

"I saw some kind of a hatching chamber. At least one of them, there may be more. There were thousands of eggs in there. Maybe even tens of thousands. The eggs were *hatching*. And from what I understand they're able to reach maturity in a matter of months as opposed to years like us. Probably another adaptation designed to quickly build up their population numbers. But think about it, Adam, in six months to a year, there could be tens, maybe even hundreds, of thousands of these creatures."

"And we're trapped in here with them," Adam said. His eyes scanned the chamber they were in. "We've got to figure out a way out of here so that we can warn the outside world."

"How? You said they killed everyone."

"I left Yeardley back at the town. She knows what's going on and where we were headed. When the sheriff and his volunteers don't come back, she'll know to contact the state troopers or the military. Someone will come."

27

The swollen moon hung heavily in the desert sky.

After waiting until nightfall, Billy and Howler had military crawled across the ground until they got back to the site of the massacre. The moonlight provided just enough illumination for them to make out things around them but not so much that they could be easily spotted.

Smoke rose from the husks of burned-out vehicles. The smell of blood and carnage still lingered in the air. There were dozens of bodies of dead and dismembered humans scattered about.

"I'm gonna be sick," groaned Howler.

"We gotta stay calm and focused, man," said Billy.

Just then Billy spotted the silhouettes of the returning gargoyles as they glided across the full moon.

"Get back down," Billy whispered sharply. "They're coming back."

Both teens fell flat to the ground and froze. They flattened out their bodies and pressed their faces into the sand. They both knew that if even one of the gargoyles saw movement it might fly down to investigate. They could hear the beating of dozens of pairs of wings as the colony flew overhead. It seemed to take an eternity for all of them to pass over.

Waiting a full thirty seconds after the last of the creatures had cleared, Billy chanced looking up. He and Howler watched as the gargoyles headed toward the opening at the base of the Tower.

Before entering, the creatures executed a banking maneuver, then flew into the mouth of the cave.

Billy and Howler rolled over onto their backs and stared straight up into the cloudless night sky.

"I don't even wanna think about what happened back in town," Howler lamented.

"We can't," said Billy.

"Everybody's probably dead, you know that."

"I know."

Howler sat up. "Man, we've gotta get the hell outta here."

"And go where?" Billy asked, sitting up as well.

"I don't know."

"We can't go back to town, some of them might still there."

"Maybe we can make it to Carson Flats."

"There's thirty miles of desert between here and there. And if those things see us, they'll pick us off like rabbits. They live in caves, so they might even be able to see in the dark."

"We could walk our bikes for a couple of miles, then start 'em up when we're far enough away. We could ride without lights."

At that moment, three gargoyles flew out of the cave opening.

"Damn, get back down!" Billy said.

The two hunkered down and froze again. The gargoyles flew over the site of the battle, their night-vision-enhanced eyes scanning. Satisfied that none of the humans were alive, the creatures split off in different directions.

Billy's and Howler's eyes followed the flying creatures until they were tiny specks.

Howler started to get up, but Billy grabbed him.

"No, just stay here and keep still," Billy whispered.

Several long minutes passed in stillness. It was nearly fifteen minutes before the gargoyles returned and regrouped. One after another, they flew back into the cave.

"That's what I was worried about. They're flying some kind of patrol," Billy guessed. "Probably seeing if there are any more people coming. If they keep doing that every hour or two, we ain't gonna be able to ride, walk, or even crawl out of here without being spotted."

"Man, aw, man." Howler felt hopeless and helpless. "Sooner or later them things are gonna spot us, and when they do they're gonna kill us."

"Howler, you gotta calm down, man. And keep your voice *low!*"

Howler lowered his voice to an anxious whisper. "What are we gonna do, Billy?"

Even when they were young, Billy had always been the natural leader. He looked to where the patrol gargoyles had reentered cave; then his eyes scanned over the scattered weapons and ammunition all around them. "Maybe we can try another strategy."

"What?"

"We go after *them.*"

"The hell! Are you crazy? What are you talkin' about?"

Billy pointed around. "Look at all these weapons lying around out here."

"Yeah, but a lotta good it did everybody."

"That's because they were sitting ducks."

"And we aren't?"

"Most folks thought this whole thing was a joke, drivin' out here lookin' for giant bats. They didn't know what to expect."

"How are we s'posed to do any better? Even with all this stuff. Did you see how big those things were? How many there were?"

"I'm not talking about fightin' 'em." He pointed in the direction of the cave opening. "See up there? There's only one entrance into that cave."

"So?"

"If we can close up that entrance, we can *trap* them things in there?"

"How the hell are we supposed to do that, man?"

"I know some folks like Larry and Carl Junior had grenades and stuff. We can use that."

"You can't be serious. You're talking about going right up to their front door and chuckin' in grenades? That's suicide!"

"Not if we catch 'em by surprise. If we blow up that cave entrance we can trap their asses behind a few thousand tons of rock, and they won't be able to get out. Then we can call in the army, National Guard, or whoever."

Howler was terrified of the thought. "I don't know, man?"

"What other choice we got?" Billy asked angrily. "Look Howl, if we try to get away, them things are gonna spot us. If we wait here doing nothing, eventually they're gonna find us."

Howler said nothing. His eyes searched around as he tried to come up with some kind of alternative plan. He couldn't. "All right, man, don't look like we got no other choice."

They cautiously got to their feet.

"Okay, first we gotta look around an' see what's around here," Billy said.

They kept crouched down as they moved through the area looking for discarded weapons.

Within a couple of minutes, Howler found a loaded automatic pistol and tucked it in his belt. Next he picked a TEC-9 submachine gun. Then he spotted what he was hoping for. "Found some grenades!" he whispered over.

The seven grenades were inside a camouflage green, multipocketed vest being worn by a dismembered torso. Howler looked away as he gingerly unzipped the blood-splattered vest. He pulled it off the torso and placed it on himself.

Billy saw a toolbox-sized green case lying beside an overturned pickup truck. Stamped on the outside was "C-4" in yellow military style stencil lettering. He popped the two latches and opened the case. Inside were four bricks of the plastic explosives, detonator caps, and a digital timer. Printed on the inside of the top lid was a diagram along with basic instructions.

"Howler, look at this," Billy whispered.

Howler crouch-ran over. "Whatcha got?"

"This is what they use in movies."

"C-4? Do you even know how to use that stuff?"

Billy held up the lid. "There's instructions right here. This is gonna work."

Billy scanned the ground and saw a camouflage backpack. He emptied out the shotgun shells and slid the case inside.

"This'll make it easier to carry," he said as he hoisted the pack onto his back.

Howler noticed something else sticking halfway out from beneath the Jeep. The green, hard shell plastic case was four feet long and about eight inches wide. Printed in the same yellow stencil type was the name "Suzy." Howler popped the twin latches on the case that had belonged to Carl Junior.

"Whoa, lookit this," he whistled.

The case contained a portable shoulder-mounted rocket launcher along with two shells. As with the C-4, the instructions were printed on the lid.

"Somebody was stocking up to fight World War III all by himself," Howler whispered. He pulled the weapon out of the case and slung the strap over his shoulder.

"What are you doin'?" Billy asked.

"I ain't going up there without it," Howler snapped back.

"All right fine," Billy agreed. "Now let's move."

Howler fit one of the shells into the launcher and put the other one in Billy's pack.

Just as the two were about to leave, they noticed something move about forty feet away from them. They crouched down defensively.

"What's that?" Howler asked.

Billy constricted his eyes. "I think somebody still alive over there."

They crouch-ran over to see who it was.

Billy reached down and rolled the person over. He immediately recognized the face. "LB?"

The deputy looked up at Billy and Howler, his eyes wide with fear.

"Them-them things killed everybody," LB said, still in a state of shock.

"What about you? You hurt bad?" asked Billy.

Howler looked the deputy up and down and didn't see any visible wounds or bleeding. "He don't look hurt at all."

"LB, how'd you survive man?"

"Ain't it obvious, he must have chickened and played dead."

"There wasn't nothin' I could do," LB said defensively.

"You're the friggin' deputy. You're supposed to preserve and protect," Howler accused.

Billy put a hand on Howler's chest, holding him back. "Back off, Howl. It was pandemonium. Everybody was scared. If LB'd tried to fight he'd have just got killed too."

LB got to his feet. "What about you two?"

"We cut when all hell broke loose. A couple of 'em chased us," Billy said. "By the time we circled back, it was too late."

"Afterwards, we also saw a pack of 'em fly off towards town," Howler added.

"That don't mean—"

"You know what it means, man?" Howler asked. "Everybody's probably dead just like here."

Billy pointed to the butte. "But when they came back, they flew into that cave at the bottom of the Tower. That's where they hole up."

"And that's where we're gonna trap 'em," said Howler, now more confident of the plan.

"Do what?" LB asked.

"We're gonna blow the cave entrance," Billy said.

"You gonna do what?"

"We got grenades and C-4," Howler added. "We can bring the whole goddamned place down on them."

"That's just stupid. The better plan is to go get help."

"Where we gonna go, LB?" Billy asked. "Carson's thirty miles away. Those things are flying out on patrols. They'll spot us before we make it a mile."

"And I checked some of the cars," Howler added. "Radios are all smashed. Them man-bats ain't stupid."

"In other words, we don't have a bunch of options. Those things could go out on another patrol at any minute. We're running out of time."

"So you got two choices, Deputy Dawg, you help us seal them bastards in or stay here and keep playin' dead like a coward."

"I ain't no coward, punk!" LB spat back, teeth clenched.

Howler shoved a shotgun into the deputy's hands. "Then prove it, dickweed!

The two men's bickering was interrupted by the sound of a groan.

"What the hell now—" LB grumbled.

There was another groan. They spotted the dark blob of a body about twenty yards away. They could see someone trying to get up to a crawl, then collapse back down.

"There's somebody else alive out here," Billy whispered.

"Another one?" said Howler.

Billy crouch-ran the twenty yards over. "Who's that?" he whispered when he got closer.

There was another groan.

Billy got to the man and took him by the shoulder to help. "You okay?"

"Billy? Billy Lightfoot?" asked a disoriented Slim.

"Yeah, yeah, it's me. You gotta quiet down, Slim."

The tanker driver was bleeding from his nose and both ears and was coughing up blood. His breathing was labored. One of his legs was cocked at a strange angle, and the broken bone could be seen poking through.

"I thought you was dead like everybody else," Billy said.

"Might as well be. One of 'em picked me up and dropped me out the air like a sack o' potatoes. Busted me all up inside."

Howler and LB came up.

"What's goin' on here?" Howler asked.

"It's Slim," said Billy.

"Hey, Slim. You okay."

"Do I look okay? Ribs feel like somebody broke a glass bottle all up in my chest."

He started coughing and spitting up blood again.

"Shut him up before he draws them things out here," LB insisted.

"He can't help it," Billy said angrily.

"Look, if we gonna try your plan, we gotta go now."

"What about Slim?"

"We can come back for him later."

Slim coughed. He looked as if he would pass out again. "Don't leave me out here."

"If those things come back out, they'll spot him for sure," Billy said.

"Then hide him somewhere! Hurry up!" LB hissed.

Billy looked around. "Howler, here help me get him over there to his truck."

Billy hooked under the man's arms, and Howler took the legs. They quickly dragged the moaning Slim over to the tanker and propped him up against the front wheel where he would be out of sight.

Howler put the man's CAT cap on his head. "You just hold on here, Slim, and watch for the fireworks."

Slim had already lost consciousness.

28

Three warrior gargoyles landed on the ledge and entered the chamber where the humans were being held.

Adam moved protectively in front of the women. "What do you want?"

Without so much as an acknowledgement, one of the creatures moved past him and grabbed Tegan by the arm. The teenager started screaming hysterically.

"Leave her alone!" Adam demanded.

A second gargoyle pulled out a bladed weapon with an antler handle and put it to Adam's neck. Threatening and baring teeth, it growled something to him in its own language.

Tamiya grabbed Adam's arm and pulled him back. "Adam no! They'll kill you!"

The gargoyles moved behind the humans and began pushing them out of the stone cell and onto the ledge. Each of the gargoyles then grabbed a human and flew them out into the main shaft.

* * *

The colony had assembled at what appeared to be a central gathering place. The area was brightly lit by hundreds of the fire-burning sconces. Additional light and warmth came from two twenty-foot-wide fire pits. At the foot of the monumental gargoyle statue was a raised stone dais. The five-foot-high dais was roughly twenty feet long by twelve feet deep.

Seated on a simple throne at the center of the dais was the gargoyle lord, V'Akiron. To his left stood K'Urgoth, and to his immediate right was S'Narra. Two tall, thin, thinker-class gargoyles stood on either side at the far edges of the dais. Garbed in bone-white robes, the blue-skinned gargoyles served a kind of religious ceremonial role, similar to clerics. They had short, curved horns and their heads were clean-shaven except for a two-foot-long braided tendril in the back. Their three-foot wings were incapable of flight.

Assembled before the dias were the nearly eight hundred gargoyles that comprised the colony—workers, warriors, and thinkers.

"My god," Adam remarked as they landed behind the assembly.

One of the guards shoved him forward. The three humans were led through the crowd of hostile creatures. As they walked they could feel cold eyes probing them. There were hisses and snarls.

The humans were led up onto the dais and then forced to their knees before the gargoyle lord. A trembling Tegan was convinced that they were about to be sacrificed.

One of the clerics came up to the kneeling humans. "I am to speak his words in your tongue," it informed them in English.

V'Akiron stood to his feet. As he addressed the assembled subjects in the gargoyle language, the cleric translated.

"As it was with our ancestors, today humans came seeking our blood. But our warriors turned them back, and it was *their* blood that was taken!"

A chant of approval went up.

"Ours was to remain in the shadows, hidden from the humans for many more turns, until we were stronger . . . until we were more. But now that is no longer possible. The humans sought us out, and soon more will come. But we will not let them destroy us . . . not this time."

29

Just outside of the cave entrance, two sentry gargoyles stood vigilant guard. There was the sound of a low whistle as a steel bolt with a razor-sharp tip cut through the air and found its target, landing with a *SSSSHUUNK*. The sentry to the left fell back. Less than four seconds later, there was another whistle, followed by another *SSSSHUUNK*. The sentry to the right clutched at its throat.

Billy, Howler, and LB crouch-ran up to the entrance. One of the gargoyles was already dead, killed instantly when the bolt entered its eye and tore into the brain. The other was on the ground gagging on its own cerulean-colored blood and squirming in final death spasms.

Howler was still carrying the portable rocket launcher, LB had picked up a minigun, and Billy was holding his trusty crossbow.

"Damn, Lightfoot, do you sleep with that thing?" LB asked in a whisper.

"It's quiet," Billy replied.

"You oughta see him doing target practice," said Howler.

"Their eye sockets are large, and the underside of their neck is just soft meat," Billy noted. "All those bones they got on the outside don't do 'em much good if you hit 'em in one of those spots."

Howler looked around to make certain there were no other gargoyles stationed outside. "It's clear," he reported.

Billy pulled off his backpack and unzipped it. "Okay, let's do this," he said.

He began pulling out the bricks of C-4 plastic explosive.

"You know what you're doing with that stuff?" LB asked.

Billy shrugged his shoulders. "I'm just gonna follow what the instructions said."

"And get us all blown up. I learned how to set this stuff in training last year. It ain't as simple as it looks on TV. Pack this stuff too loosely or set the blasting caps wrong and either it don't work or it'll go off prematurely, taking your asses with it. Here, give it to me."

Billy handed over the backpack.

Howler unsnapped one of the pockets on his vest and pulled out a grenade. "I still don't know why we didn't just toss these in like I suggested."

"They don't pack nearly enough punch to collapse all this rock," said LB. "All you'd end up doing is makin' a lot of noise and bringin' the whole pissed-off pack down on us."

The mouth of the cave was approximately fifteen feet high and twenty-five feet wide. About a hundred years ago, the entrance had been expanded so that it could be used by a mining company exploring the cave for silver, gold, or other precious metals or valuable minerals. The effort was abandoned when the cave turned out to be bone-dry. Over the years the occasional group of spelunkers would stumbled onto the cave, but it was never a well-known or mapped destination. A couple of amateur cavers had gone missing a year ago, but no one had known where they were caving so the disappearance remained unsolved.

LB's eyes surveyed the entrance. "Keep a lookout," he instructed.

Slinging on the backpack, LB quietly and carefully climbed up along the side of the entrance. Once he reached the top, he pulled off the pack, reached into the case, and pulled out one of the C-4 bricks. He took out the small green seven-inch metal shovel that was also in the case and used it to scoop out a four-inch-deep hole in the loose dirt between the rocks. He placed the brick inside, packed the dirt tight around it, and then inserted the blasting cap and leads. The process took about five anxious minutes.

"Okay," LB announced. "First one's set."

"How many more?" Billy whispered up.

LB looked across the length of the cave. "Three more, each spaced about six feet apart just to be sure." He held up the card-deck-sized detonator switch, which had a red button in the center. "Then I just hit this to bring it all down."

"Hurry up, man," Howler whispered up to him anxiously. "Them man-bats could go back on patrol at any minute!"

"I'm goin' as fast as I can. I gotta do it right."

"Okay, okay. But this is gonna work though, right?"

"Should. Now let me do this."

LB started working his way to the next position.

Billy peered down the 250-foot-long cave and noticed the illumination from the central shaft in the far distance.

"Hey," he whispered. "There's light coming from way down there."

"Who cares, man?" Howler asked. "Probably them things. Maybe they don't live in total darkness."

Billy strained his ears. "I think I can hear voices."

"You're imagining things."

"No, listen."

Howler listened closely, and he also heard what sounded like voices rising from the central shaft and echoing in the chamber.

Billy took a few steps down the corridor to get a better look.

"Where the hell are you going, Billy?" LB demanded.

"To take a look."

"With them things down there?" Howler cried.

"Lightfoot, get back here," the deputy ordered. "We got work to do."

"You gonna risk getting us caught, man," Howler agreed.

"I'm tellin' you I can hear voices down there," Billy said. "That means there could be somebody alive in there."

"No, there ain't."

"There's voices and them things can't talk. We saw 'em take that professor guy. Maybe that's him calling for help."

"Billy, there ain't nobody in there but them things."

Billy stepped back to outside the entrance. Pacing, he looked up at LB who was working on the setting the second explosive.

"How much longer, LB?"

"Twelve, maybe fifteen minutes," the deputy informed.

Billy couldn't take it anymore. "I'm gonna take a look."

"What the hell is with you? There ain't nobody in there. And even if there was, there's nothin' we can do. Either they're dead or as good as."

"We don't know that."

"For christsakes, Billy," Howler complained. "If anything them things probably eat people."

"I'm still gonna check it out," Billy said stubbornly. "I gotta."

"Lightfoot, I said stop, goddammit," LB ordered. "I'm still the law."

Bill looked at the star-shaped badge on the deputy's rumpled, dirt-covered shirt. "What are you gonna do, arrest me?"

"Listen up, Billy," LB informed. "I swear to god, once I get this all set, I'm blowin' it. Whether you're out here or not."

Billy didn't reply. Instead he started into the cave.

"Whoa, whoa, whoa," Howler whispered. "C'mon, Billy, them things could be up in the ceiling hanging upside down like bats. What if you set 'em off."

Billy scanned the ceiling. "There's nothing between here and that light," he whispered back.

He continued moving forward in a low crouch.

Struggling with his own conscience, Howler watched his friend for several seconds. "Son of a . . ." he cursed himself. "Wait up."

Howler caught up. "You're a stubborn ass fool, but somebody's gotta watch your back."

30

"When the humans learn what has happened this day more will come," the gargoyle lord warned. "But they will find nothing. Tomorrow we will burn the bodies. Then we will return here to the shadows . . . and wait and grow in number. With every passing day, more of our hatchlings emerge. In another cycle of the moon, there will be five thousand more . . . By the next cycle ten thousand. And our hatchlings will grow quickly and strong."

Another cheer went up.

Six hundred feet above, Billy and Howler were lying on their stomachs and looking over the lip of the cave into the central shaft.

"Man, this is like somethin' outta a horror movie," whispered Howler. "There's a whole goddamned nest of 'em down there. And they *can* talk. That one's talkin' in some kinda language."

Billy spotted Adam, Tamiya, and Tegan, who were on their knees in front of the gargoyle lord. "Look." He pointed. "There they are! Three of 'em."

"Yeah," Howler observed. "Surrounded by a hundreds of them damned man bats. Look at 'em all. Jeezus."

Howler started to get up to head back. Billy grabbed his arm. "Hold on."

"Billy man, there ain't nothing we can do for them folks. And LB ain't gonna wait, you know that."

"We seal them in here with those things, and you know they won't stand a chance."

"What choice do we got?"

"We need to go back and tell LB there's people alive in here. Then figure somethin' out."

"Are you crazy? That boy is scared shitless. He ain't gonna stop. Not for us . . . not for them."

"You're talkin' about leavin' people down there, Howler. Two women."

"I feel bad for 'em too, but we ain't got no choice. Look at all them things down there. There ain't a thing we can do." Howler was frantic.

Billy looked around, assessing the situation. He saw that the three humans were being guarded by only one of the warriors. There was also a robed blue gargoyle with small wings that appeared to be speaking directly to them.

"How many grenades you got?" he asked.

"I don't know." Howler patted the pockets on the vest. "Six, no seven all together. But, man . . ."

Billy grabbed out two of the grenades. Then he looked at the portable rocket launcher slung over Howler's shoulder. "How about that thing?"

"One shell in the barrel plus the extra."

"That's more'n enough to create a diversion."

"What?"

Billy's eyes panned the carved-in stairs that spiraled along the inside of the shaft. Too many. Too exposed.

However, there were other passageways cut into the shaft. At four locations around the shaft, there were sets of stairs carved out just inside the walls, which were designed to accommodate the flightless gargoyles. The steps went straight down, with flights alternating back and forth like in a parking garage. One of the entry points was about thirty feet away from them. That route let out at the bottom, less than fifty feet from the dais.

Billy pointed to the lower exit. "I can make my way down there."

"Dude, LB's gonna . . ."

"Shouldn't take more than two or three minutes for me to get down there. Then once I'm in place—"

"Yeah, yeah I know, open up a can of grenade whup-ass on 'em. But you still ain't gonna make it back up in time."

"I can make it. Grab them folks in the confusion and get back. But if I don't, you haul your ass outta here before LB blows the cave."

Billy started to military crawl over toward the opening. Howler grabbed his arm and looked his friend in the eyes.

"Billy, man, why you goin' down in that snake pit with all those things? You don't even know them people."

Billy shouldered his crossbow. "I couldn't help that girl the other night," he admitted. "I ain't forgot the look in her eyes when they carried her off."

31

"We are an ancient race." V'Akiron's voice rose up through the chamber. He was on his feet. "Our ancestors were here for many cycles. While we slept the humans only continued to spread. But soon our kind will take back what is ours!"

Nearly three minutes had passed when Howler finally saw Billy appear down below where the stairs let out. He was tucked in behind the inner rock wall. Being so close to the throngs of gargoyles, Billy could feel fear and anxiety clenching in his chest. However, he knew that the clock was ticking. He closed his eyes to compose himself, then looked up to where Howler was crouched, barely able to make out the small head so far away.

"Remember this night my brothers . . . my sisters . . . my children," the gargoyle lord proclaimed. "This night marks the end of the reign of man and the beginning of the reign of gargoyle!"

A raucous cheer rose up from the colony.

At that, Billy signaled to Howler.

Howler pulled the pin and tossed in the first grenade.

There was a *TINK, TINK, TINK* as the incendiary grenade bounced off rocks on its way down. Several of the gargoyles stopped when they heard the clinking sounds. Their eyes turned to the apple-sized metal object as it landed on the dirt floor right in the center of the crowd. It lay there for a second . . . then exploded.

A powerful, concussive blast tore through the assembly of gargoyles, sending hot gases and shrapnel in all directions. The incendiary effects scorched bodies, and metal tore through limbs. At least five gargoyles were killed instantly, and several more were severely injured.

Less than five seconds later, a second grenade landed. A second explosion. More carnage.

Then a third grenade.

A fourth.

A fifth.

Explosions were going off everywhere. Terror and confusion raced through the colony like wildfire. Dozens upon dozens of the creatures were dead, and scores more were wounded and bloodied. Body parts lay everywhere. A thick fog of smoke and dust rose up in the shaft.

In the pandemonium, Adam, Tamiya, and Tegan were trying to make sense of what was happening. A crossbow bolt whistled through the air and struck the cleric gargoyle guarding them between its horns, entering the creature's brain and killing it instantly.

Billy emerged from the thick clouds of smoke and dust at the foot of the dais. He was frantically motioning to them. "Professor! Girls! C'mon!" he called.

The unguarded humans wasted no time in scrambling to their feet to follow their rescuer. Tamiya grabbed Tegan by the arm and pulled her along with them.

Out of grenades, Howler was on his feet with the rocket launcher perched on his shoulder, his eye to the scope, "Hey, you goddamned man-bats!" he yelled down.

The gargoyles looked up.

"A human!" K'Urgoth pointed.

It was like shooting at fish in a barrel. Howler fired the weapon, launching a nine-inch rocket down into the shaft. The recoil of the weapon knocked him off his feet and to the ground.

V'Akiron's eyes widened as the shell headed toward the dais, trailing a plume of white-and-gray smoke. He knew what it meant. "No!"

A split second later, the shell impacted.

The concussive explosion was several times more powerful than the grenades. It sent gargoyle bodies flying in all directions. Large chunks of rock and huge boulders tumbled down, pummelling and crushing the fleeing creatures.

It took nearly five seconds for the reverberations to stop, and another ten seconds for the smoke to begin dissipating. There were ripped body parts, limbs, and large chunks of seared flesh strewn about everywhere. Severely injured gargoyles were moaning and screaming.

K'Urgoth moved through turmoil, his eyes desperately searching for the attacker at the top of the shaft. He was bleeding profusely from a gash on his forehead and a deep laceration across his chest. One of his horns was raggedly broken nearly in half and the right side of his face was seared with second-and third-degree burns.

Howler scrambled back up to his feet and placed in the second rocket.

"Kill the human creature!" the warrior gargoyle barked. "Bring me its head!"

Howler aimed and fired. This time he had braced for the recoil. The second rocket, though slightly off target, was devastating nonetheless. The explosion indiscriminately ripped through the bodies of male, female, and young gargoyles of every caste. Scores more were killed.

The gargoyles were in total disarray and blinded by smoke, terror, and grief.

Billy was trying to rapidly lead Adam, Tamiya, and Tegan up the steps. The passage was less than five feet wide, with smooth stone on either side and only nominal illumination from the small torches set at each landing. Each flight was roughly thirty feet long and rose at a steep sixty-five degree angle. This made it necessary for them to scramble up using their hands and feet in a somewhat crawling fashion. Racing against time, they had already managed to climb four of the ten flights.

K'Urgoth began gathering any available warriors to try to mount a counterattack. "It is only one human," he said. "Attack it from different directions."

Following the orders, the warriors took to the air.

Out of grenades and rockets, Howler switched to the TEC-9. He began firing down, attempting to take out the gargoyles before they could get off the ground.

Billy figured that they probably had maybe three or four minutes left before LB detonated the C-4, provided he didn't finish early, in which case, Billy knew the deputy wouldn't hesitate for one second, especially after hearing all the commotion.

Just then Adam heard skittering noises coming from about forty feet behind them. He looked back to see about twenty of the small, wingless, worker gargoyles heading their way.

"Billy!" Adam yelled ahead.

Billy looked back and saw the scurrying creatures. "Holy shit! How many?"

"A lot of 'em!"

Reflective eyes wide, sharp teeth and fangs bared, the enraged worker gargoyles were chasing down the humans like a pack of rabid rats.

Billy slowed and pushed Tamiya and Tegan ahead. "Go! Go! Professor, take the women and keep movin'!"

"What about you?"

Billy pulled the grenades out of his pockets. "I gotta surprise for the little bastards."

The five warrior gargoyle flying up the shaft were crisscrossing and randomizing their flight vectors, making it difficult for Howler to target them. He was firing in short bursts—*tat-tat-tat, tat-tat-tat, tat-tat-tat*. They were already a third of the way up and closing fast.

He took out one and watched as its wings went limp, and the creature fell spiraling back down the shaft. Down to four. Two hundred feet away.

Several bullets bounced off the tough exoskeleton of another gargoyle, but a second volley of bullets tore through its right wing, shredding it like a World War I biplane. Down to three. One hundred feet away.

Howler concentrated his fire on a bald gargoyle with a ragged facial scar. Bullets ripped into the creature's face and chest. Down to two. Fifty feet away.

Aiming for another warrior, Howler squeezed the trigger again. Nothing. The 32-round magazine was empty.

"Dammit!" he shouted in frustration.

Two gargoyles were twenty-five feet away and closing in for the kill. One carried a double-bladed axe.

"C'mon! C'mon!" Howler shook the automatic weapon, trying to will it back to life. He pulled out the smoking clip. It was empty, and he knew he didn't have a replacement.

Twenty feet . . . He was out of weapons. Fifteen feet . . . Ten . . .

Closing his eyes, Howler braced himself for the death blow.

There was a mechanical WHIRRRRR, and an explosion of sound from behind Howler. The warriors were blown back as high-caliber slugs tore through their wings, muscle, and internal organs.

A rattled Howler spun around.

"Your fifteen minutes were up!" LB grumbled.

He was holding a smoking six-barreled minigun.

"Dude, you just saved my butt," Howler sighed in relief and gratitude.

"Just be happy I didn't leave you. Where the hell's Lightfoot?"

"On his way back up. He's got the professor and two of them college girls."

"Well, he'd better haul ass! C-4's set and ready to blow!"

"You don't have to tell me twice."

"C'mon, let's get the hell outta—"

Before LB could finish his sentence, a warrior gargoyle swooped down out of the shadows like a dark angel of death. Wings spread wide with razor bone blades out.

In a flash, the deputy was decapitated. LB's severed head fell forward, his knees buckled, and his burly body toppled to the ground.

"Jeezus!" Howler cried out in shock.

Gliding like a stealth killer, the warrior silently circled around to set up for a second attack run. Howler's eyes darted from the incoming warrior to the fallen minigun. He dove onto the gun and quickly scooped it up in his hands. Still on his knees, Howler screamed as he opened fire.

Hot slugs zipped through the air. Hit numerous times, the gargoyle bucked and jerked as it was blown back.

Silence.

Only seconds later, Adam, Tamiya, Tegan, and Billy emerged from the passageway.

"Howler!" Billy called out.

Wide-eyed, Howler turned around. His expression turned to one of relief. "Billy, you made it man!"

At the bottom of the shaft, K'Urgoth watched the last of the warriors he'd sent up, come crashing to the ground. The hulking gargoyle's primal roar echoed throughout the entire chamber.

As he started toward Howler, Billy saw LB's decapitate body on the ground. "What happened?"

"He came in after us. Saved my life, man," Howler explained. "Then one of them things kilt him."

Billy was both stunned and saddened. He had misjudged LB, and now they all owed the deputy their lives.

"He said he set the C-4, we just gotta blow it."

K'Urgoth had gathered sixteen winged workers that had survived and were still healthy enough to fly. They were obediently gathered at his feet, looking up.

"Swarm!" he commanded.

Like vicious vampire bats, the small gargoyles took to the air.

The furious drumming of wings were heard seconds before the first of the flying goblins appeared over the shaft edge.

Tegan screamed. Howler turned the minigun and opened fire. Lacking the warrior's thick exoskeleton, the workers were much easier to kill, and two of them were struck immediately. Their bodies blasted apart like melons splattering gore in every direction. However, the workers were agile flyers and were able to quickly disperse in all directions. Then they all turned back around and were surrounding him from multiple directions, hissing and snarling.

Howler realized what he was up against. They were coordinating their attack.

He slapped Billy on the back. "Go!" he yelled. "I'll take care of these little bastards."

Billy looked into his friend's eyes.

"Go, man," Howler said simply.

Billy grabbed Tegan's hand and pulled her in the direction of the cave opening. Adam and Tamiya followed.

Minigun fire erupted again. The workers swarmed like piranha, attacking from various angles. One of the creatures managed to get behind Howler, clamping onto the back of his thigh and sinking in its three-quarter-inch, razor-sharp fangs. Another bit into his right forearm. Then another got through and latched onto his neck. Howler was thrown off balance, and the gunfire went in a wild arc off target. This created the opening that the others needed. Within seconds, they were all upon him, teeth and claws tearing into flesh.

Having gotten everyone about fifty feet away, Billy chanced a quick look back. He was horrified to see his friend mercilessly swarmed by the small gargoyles. He could hear Howler's cries of pain as the ravenous creatures tore away at his flesh.

Tears welled in Billy's eyes as he reluctantly followed the professor. The girls were a few feet ahead, making their way to the exit.

Tamiya was the first to spot K'Urgoth rising up over the central shaft. He was joined by the two remaining warriors on either side.

"There's more of them!" she cried.

Running as fast as they could, they headed straight for the opening of the cave, which was less than one hundred yards away.

Billy was just behind Adam. "The entrance is wired with C-4," he yelled. "We just need to hit the detonator to blow it."

The gargoyles were closing in fast. K'Urgoth was in the lead. The cave entrance was still sixty yards away. It was going to be close.

"They're gaining!" Adam reported.

Fifty yards to the entrance. They could hear the beating of the wings behind them.

Tamiya took a quick glance back. "Oh god, we're not gonna make it!"

She was right.

Suddenly, two blinding circular lights appeared in front of them.

"What . . ." Adam started to say.

A horn blared as the propane tanker truck entered the mouth of the cave. Inside, Slim was slumped over the wheel, gravely injured but still in control of the vehicle.

"Get to the sides!" Adam yelled.

Everyone moved out of the way, clearing a path for the tanker. Billy pulled Tegan over to the right, Adam and Tamiya went to the left. The tanker barreled by them, going roughly thirty-five miles an hour.

Startled by the oncoming vehicle and temporarily blinded by the light, two of the gargoyles still managed to move out of the way just in time. A third was not so lucky. The tanker rammed into it head-on, crumpling it over the hood.

The tanker continued on, picking up speed as Slim had the gas pedal pushed all the way down. It was headed directly toward the central shaft and a three-hundred-foot drop.

The truck broke over the ledge and sailed out into the open shaft like a stunt car. Then the heavier weight nose end of the vehicle took over and the tanker angled downward.

Adam, Tamiya, Tegan, and Billy scrambled back to their feet and began desperately running and stumbling toward the exit about forty yards away.

"That truck's filled with propane," Billy said. "When it hits—"

He didn't have to say anything more.

The two remaining gargoyles were also regrouping. Talking a running start, they leapt off the ground and spread their wings to once again pursue the fleeing humans.

The propane tanker plunged headlong toward the floor of the shaft.

Inside the cab, Slim swore with his dying words, "I'm sendin' y'all demons straight back ta hell!"

The truck hit the bottom, exploding on impact.

Thirty-five hundred gallons of propane ignited, forming a huge fireball that filled the shaft. Any gargoyles at ground zero were instantly incinerated.

Twenty-five yards from the opening.
The gargoyles were fifty yards behind and closing.

The fireball rose up, filling the shaft, the hatcheries, all the chambers—consuming everything within.

Fifteen yards away.
The gargoyles had closed to within twenty-five yards.

Intense heat and licking flames began filling the exit corridor. The gargoyle furthest back was engulfed by the twenty-five-hundred-degree blue-and-yellow flames. It let out a scream as it was cremated alive.

Five yards away.
The flames caught and encircled K'Urgoth. His skin blistered, boiled, and blackened before being completely enveloped.

The four humans cleared the exit just in time, racing to the sides as the cave belched out a long torrent of flames. The heat triggered the C-4, setting off a succession of tremendous explosions. Chunks of rock blew apart and tons of massive boulders tumbled down.

The superheated air rumbled thunderously, and the ground shook violently both from the explosions and falling rocks.

It took nearly two minutes for the rumbling and shaking to stop and the last of the flames to die down. When it was over, the mouth of the cave had completely collapsed. If any of the creatures had somehow managed to survive, they were now buried alive under thousands of tons of rock.

32

The four survivors lay on the ground outside the cave, completely drained from the ordeal. Their bodies were covered with ash and dirt. The acrid smell of propane still lingered in the air.

Adam was the first to stir. "Tam, are you okay?"

"We made it," she replied. "We made it."

They both slowly got to their feet.

Tegan sat up, her back pressed against a large boulder. "Are we safe now? Is it over?"

"Yes," Adam replied. "It's over."

Billy was limping in their direction. As the last person out, he hadn't quite escaped injury. The blue-hot flames had scorched through his shirt, blistering his back, right shoulder, and triceps with second-degree burns. His right calf was also severely burned.

"Billy, you're hurt," Tamiya said with concern.

"I'll be okay," he grunted.

Tegan flung herself into the young Navajo, wrapping her arms around him in gratitude. "You came! You came for me."

"Ye-up."

"I can never thank you enough," Adam said.

"What the hell were those things, professor?"

"They're called gargoyles."

Billy looked at the collapsed cave entrance. The cloud of dust and smoke was slowly beginning to settle. "Well if there's any of them damned demons left alive, their asses are trapped in there. So what now?"

"We need to contact the authorities. Tell them what happened and have them take charge of this place."

"Like the state po-po?"

"More like the military and the government."

"Yeah, I s'pose that makes—"

Without explanation, Billy suddenly tensed up.

"Billy?" Adam asked.

The young man's eyes were wide and vacantly stared out into nowhere. His mouth was agape and trying to work, but all he could emit were gagging and gurgling sounds.

A dark red stain began expanding outward from the center of Billy's blue denim shirt. The crossbow dropped from his hand.

Tamiya started backing away, pulling a confused and horrified Tegan with her.

Billy's chest bucked outward as the sharp tail blade broke completely through and protruded out six inches. It dripped with blood.

Tegan let out a siren-pitched wail.

Billy was slowly lifted two feet off the ground, his legs dangling. He was spasming, gagging, and spitting up blood. Then his legs began trembling, and his eyes rolled back.

The figure in the shadow behind him came into full view. V'Akiron!

The gargoyle lord towered over the humans. There were cuts, burns, and abrasions covering its blue-scaled body. Thick, phosphorescent bright-blue blood flowed from several open wounds.

Whipping his powerful tail, V'Akiron effortlessly flicked aside the dead human.

"Murderers," the gargoyle lord accused as he came toward the humans, dragging a knarled leg behind him. "Everything destroyed . . . my colony . . . my family."

Adam backed away but kept himself protectively between the gargoyle and the women. "We were only defending ourselves. You slaughtered dozens of innocent people."

"And you murdered hundreds! Thousands more unhatched!"

"You would have killed us. You abducted and killed my students . . ."

"You were the trespassers! The old one took one of our dead."

"The old . . . Joe? We didn't know."

V'Akiron hissed, "It did not matter! It is what your kind has always done—hunted and destroyed my kind—males . . . females . . . hatchlings."

Eyes blazing with hatred and fury, the large gargoyle started to lunge toward Adam.

"Stop!" warned Tamiya. She was standing ten feet to the right and holding the crossbow leveled directly at the gargoyle lord's chest. Her hands were trembling as she looked up at the large creature. "Don't—don't take another step."

"You think that will stop me?" the gargoyle lord asked defiantly.

"Ask the gargoyles it's already killed."

"Tam, get away from him," Adam said.

"I know what I'm doing, Adam."

Unexpectantly another voice came from behind them.

"Stop or I kill her," S'Narra threatened.

They turned around to see the female gargoyle holding Tegan from behind; her long clawed fingers were clasped around the teen's throat.

Tamiya answered the threat with one of her own. "Let her go or I swear I'll shoot him."

The female gargoyle hissed, then tightened her grasp, digging claws into Tegan's neck and drawing blood. Tegan let out a whimper.

Tamiya fired the crossbow. A razor-tipped steel bolt plunged four inches into the gargoyle lord's left chest.

V'Akiron howled in pain.

S'Narra screeched in shock at seeing her leader shot by the human.

Hands trembling, Tamiya quickly grabbed another bolt and placed it in the slot.

"Tell that bitch to let her go!" she yelled to V'Akiron.

The injured gargoyle lord was hunched over. He was breathing heavily like a wounded bull. Cerulean blood streamed down his chest from the newly opened wound. His eyes narrowed in hatred.

"Then kill me, human," V'Akiron dared defiantly.

"No!" S'Narra yanked Tegan's long blonde hair and held her razor-sharp claws to the teen's neck. "I kill her!"

"Stop!" Adam yelled.

Everyone froze.

Adam looked into V'Akiron's eyes. "How many of your species have died today? Hundreds. Thousands more unborn. There may be some in there who survived but not likely. Now it's just the two of you left."

"Because of you!" V'Akiron growled.

"Because we didn't communicate."

Adam's eyes softened. "All of this could have been avoided. All of this tragedy and death on both sides. You are an intelligent species. An important species that we didn't even know existed. Imagine the things we could learn about your biology, your culture, your language. Whatever history your species might have had with humans is in the past. We are not our ancestors of five hundred years ago."

"You are still humans." V'Akiron retorted. "Your kind would gather us like animals, keep us in cages like slaves, hold us up as demons?"

Adam reluctantly realized that V'Akiron might be right. He could easily imagine the gargoyles being shackled and taken to a government facility. There would be tests and experiments. Eventually the creatures would either be hidden away in a prison or put on display in some kind of a zoo. Once people learned about the existence of real living gargoyles there would be everything from curiosity seekers to religious fundamentalists parading them about as proof of angels and devils, heaven and hell.

"It would be better to kill us now," said V'Akiron.

Adam considered this for several long moments, then said, "No, it wouldn't."

Tamiya was alarmed. "Why not?"

Adam looked at his girlfriend. "Because it's genocide. They're the last two left alive, Tam."

"They're monsters, Adam!"

"And we're scientists. We should know better."

"They killed the boys."

"And now she has Tegan, Tam! I'm not going to lose another student. And I'm not going to be responsible for the extinction of a species just at the moment we discover them."

"Then what the hell are you saying?"

Adam looked first at the gargoyle lord, who regarded him with suspicion and simmering anger. Tamiya still had the crossbow trained on him and aimed at the neck. Adam then looked at S'Narra who was holding the terrified Tegan. Tears were streaming down the teen's face. The female gargoyle could rip out her throat or crush her neck with little effort.

"We're at a stalemate," Adam said, looking directly into V'Akiron's eyes.

The gargoyle looked away in contempt.

"But we can break it."

Still refusing eye contact. "Speak."

"Tell her to release my student, and we'll let the two of you leave."

"Adam, what are you doing?" Tamiya was sure he had lost his mind.

V'Akiron turned his eyes to Adam. "I do not trust you."

"Trust is the only thing we have left." Adam looked out into the desert, which stretched on for as far as the eye could see. "You can survive out there and find another hiding place and start another colony."

"Adam, are you insane?" Tamiya asked.

"Tam, please."

"S'Narra is not a breeder," V'Akiron said. "My colony has ended."

"But at least you'll be alive and free."

V'Akiron looked at Adam, studying the human's face. He looked at Tamiya, who was still aiming the crossbow at him with fierce determination. Then he looked at S'Narra and Tegan.

Finaly, the gargoyle lord said something to S'Narra in their language. She protested. He barked another order, and she reluctantly relaxed her grip.

"Tam?" Adam said.

"I hope you know what you're doing." Tamiya lowered the crossbow a little but not enough to give the creature an opening.

Still holding Tegan, S'Narra moved over beside the injured V'Akiron. Once the gargoyles were together, the female pushed Tegan over to Adam and Tamiya.

Without so much as a word, V'Akiron and S'Narra opened their broad wings and, with one powerful flap, propelled themselves into the sky.

The humans watched as the two gargoyles flew off. Wings flapping rhythmically, the creatures grew smaller and smaller with each passing second.

33

The gargoyles had flown perhaps three hundred yards when, inexplicably, V'Akiron stopped. He executed a wide, banking turn and headed back in the direction of the humans.

Seeing the creature returning, Adam narrowed his eyes. "What the hell is he doing?"

"I knew it!" cursed Tamiya. She hoisted the crossbow back up.

A still terrified Tegan shrank back.

V'Akiron came to a stop about twenty-five feet away. Flapping its wings, the gargoyle lord hovered twenty feet above them.

"You believe you have won, humans?" V'Akiron asked. "That you have destroyed us?" his reptilian eyes narrowed. "You destroyed one colony. There are many, many more. We are everywhere . . . and soon, we will emerge."

The gargoyle lord turned and flew off to rejoin the female. They both disappeared into the black, velvety void of night.

The End

Edwards Brothers Malloy
Thorofare, NJ USA
July 13, 2012